WICKED LIES

USA TODAY bestselling author

RENEE HARLESS

WICKED LIES

USA TODAY bestselling author

RENEE HARLESS

I had a new life.

One that I fought for.

One that I lied for.

One that I would do anything to protect.

No one knew about the secrets that kept me awake at night.

I fought tooth and nail to keep everyone at arm's length.

Until a woman I hadn't seen since childhood showed up on my doorstep.

Keeley Fox wanted answers, but all that I could give her were lies.

Lies that would shield her from the nastiness of my past. A past that collided with hers and could destroy the pretty world that she lived in.

One push from her became too much and I savored her downfall, except she took me down with her.

Now I was exposed to all of Wellington University and that reputation I had built was a pile of bricks at my feet.

The greatest lie of all was that love was worth the fight.

CHAPTER ONE

KEELEY

I stared down at the plastic cup filled three-quarters of the way with a bright red liquid. It wasn't anything special like what my friends had in their cups. No, mine was plain fruit punch. Drinking alcohol wasn't one of the things I took pleasure in like most college kids. I witnessed the loss of inhibitions and hangovers that followed my classmates, and that was absolutely something I had zero desire to undergo myself.

Most of the people at the party sneered at me when I turned down the shots my friends were handing out. I tried my hardest not to deflate when I heard the term "goody-two-shoes" murmured behind my back, but I had bigger things to focus on than fitting in with the crowd. I had to figure out where I was going to live.

"I am so sorry," Sarah said as she slouched onto the couch beside me, her own cup filled with spiked liquid sloshing over the edge onto her pants. She rested her head on my shoulder in what I assumed she thought was a gentle manner, but in reality, it felt like a ten-pound weight colliding with me. "I feel like the shittiest friend ever."

I didn't want to tell her that she had indeed done a really shitty thing because Sarah and I had been best friends and roommates since we both transferred to Wellington University. Now she was in love with Archer Calloway and they were taking their relationship to the next level by moving in together. I wanted to hate Archer for being the reason I was in this mess to begin with, but I couldn't bring myself to garner that emotion. They were in love, just like my friend Jolee with Archer's brother Ford.

Sarah and I had been paired randomly as roommates because we were transfer students at Wellington University last year. I had lucked out because Sarah and I immediately hit it off and were quick friends.

We met Jolee in our first business class. All three of us stood out as new students and sat together in the stadium-style room. Sarah and I had watched her relationship with Ford unfold. He was in the class and made it his mission to terrorize her on a daily basis, until he had a change of heart and fell head-over-heels for her.

The two of them had done the unthinkable and each brought a Ridge Rogue to their knees. Which was quite the feat considering the Ridge Rogues were notorious playboys and assholes around campus. I steered clear of them for the most part since drawing attention to myself was the last thing that I wanted.

I also didn't want or plan to find myself homeless with classes starting in two weeks.

"She knows that you didn't mean to throw away the lease renewal, Sarah," Jolee chimed in from my other side before tucking her foot beneath one of her legs and turning to face me. "Are you sure there isn't anyone looking for a roommate?"

"Not that I could find. I scoured through the Wellington roommate portal and looked around the boards at some of the businesses around the school. Anyone that needed a roommate has already filled their spot." I didn't need to mention that most of Wellington's students were the heirs of the upper echelon of society. Royals, hotel heirs, and mafia princes all rubbed elbows with those on scholarship, but none wanted to slum with one. Not to mention that the town of Wellington was just a blip on the map.

"So, what do you think you'll do?" Jolee asked. Shrugging my shoulders, I took a large gulp of my drink, wishing that it was more than just fruit punch this one time. Wishing that I had the luxury to let myself go for a chance.

"She can come live with us until she finds something," Sarah offered, but I immediately shook my head. I did not want to be the third wheel in her happiness. Plus, I had been witness to Sarah and Archer's *love* enough times that I still heard their groans in my sleep.

"My stuff is in storage for the time being, and I guess I'll see if I can get a last-minute placement in the dorms until an apartment opens up. Otherwise, I suppose I could move back home and transfer."

Dad was insistent that I get my business degree before becoming a partner in his trading company. I wasn't exactly sure what he traded, but it would be good to have a job waiting for me after I graduated, unlike most of my colleagues. Part of that stipulation was that I had to follow his rules, which was why I was at Wellington in the first place. Except he didn't know that I had been renting an apartment, it went against one of his crazy cohabitation rules. Anyone I was friends with back home had to go through a background check and his approval, which was why I had zero friends.

"You can't leave!" Jolee shouted as she wrapped her arm around me, her red drink sloshing over the edge of her cup and spilling onto my white shorts.

Great.

In my rush to stand up, I tipped my cup over, causing the liquid to spill down the front of my pale pink tank top. Just when I thought the day couldn't get any worse I had to go and ruin my clothes.

"Oh, Keeley, I'm so sorry," Jolee apologized profusely as I stood.

"I'll be right back." We were in one of the Ridge Rogue's apartments, the oldest one, if I wasn't mistaken. The three-bedroom apartment was similar to the one Jolee had lived in, so I easily found the bathroom and breathed a sigh of relief when it wasn't occupied. Or filthy like most men's bathrooms.

Locking the door, I turned and stared at myself in the mirror. I was a complete mess. Not just with my appearance, but with my life. If I wasn't so excited to follow the same path as my father, I wasn't quite sure what I would do with myself. There was one year remaining until I graduated and I was afraid that I wasn't quite prepared for the real world.

Glancing down at my now ruined shirt and shorts, I couldn't even bring myself to care. It wasn't like anyone at the University paid me enough mind to notice the stains on my clothes, which was made even more apparent as I stepped from the bathroom just as a group of girls ran right into me. To them, I was invisible, and it had never bothered me in the past, but now for some reason, it ignited a flame inside me.

I stomped away from the group, ignoring the giggles of the girls as I passed, and wove myself back to the living area. We were supposed to be here as a way to say goodbye to our friend Haley and the Ridge Rogue brother Rylan as they went to study abroad for a semester, but Haley was as big on crowds as I was. Which meant she hadn't left a barstool in the kitchen. And Rylan hadn't even made an appearance yet.

Most of the people in the apartment were women here to snag one of the Ridge Rogues, and as I searched the space, it seemed like they had accomplished what they came for.

I didn't think I had been in the bathroom long, but in my absence, Ford and Archer had taken up the empty seat on the couch that I vacated. A group of people occupied the other sofa in various stages of undress.

This was absolutely not my scene.

I walked into the kitchen to find Haley and let her know that I planned to leave. She had been gracious enough to let me crash at her apartment until she left in the morning. The apartment was already subleased for the semester and the renters were moving their things in tomorrow.

Perched on her stool, Haley was shooting daggers at anyone that even came close to approaching her. It would have been comical if the party wasn't for her in the first place.

"Hey," I said as I moved in her line of sight. She wore an expression that made it clear that she was ready to toss out an insult until she realized that the person invading her space was me.

Despite her dark appearance, she managed a smirk as she took in my pink stains. "Do I want to know?" she asked.

"No. Just a mishap. Anyway, I think I'm going to head back to the apartment. This isn't really my scene and I need to figure out where I'm going to stay."

"Yeah, I won't be too far behind you. It seems the Rogue chasers are out in full force," she added with a sneer as another gaggle of women stumbled into the apartment on the arms of two more of the brothers.

"You aren't wrong. Anyway, I'll see you in the morning before you leave so I can give you your key. I guess I should let Sarah and Jolee know that I'm leaving too." Looking out through the kitchen opening, I watched our friends laugh at something one of the newcomers said. Ford's laugh was boisterous as he tossed his head back, his arm tightening around Jolee's shoulder. I couldn't see who had caused him to laugh so hard, but it felt as if I was peeking into a private conversation.

"Keeley?" Haley's voice sounded far away until I realized I had been caught staring at the group that continued to grow.

"I'm sorry, what?"

"I was just saying that I'll see you in the morning."

"Oh, sure," I said.

My nerves began to quake and it escalated as I approached my ex-roommate and friend while they joked with the newcomers. I wasn't sure why, but I felt like I was the new kid in elementary school. Ten or more sets of eyes turned in my direction and I felt my mouth turning to cotton. I licked my lips, hoping that it would calm me as well as offer me the courage to speak – it did neither.

I stood there awkwardly; my palms grew sweaty at the clan of gorgeous people whose attention I had garnered. I was not a fan of crowds or attention, something my father tried to remedy by enrolling me in public speaking classes. They hadn't worked so far.

"Do you talk?" one of the long-legged blondes said as she draped herself across the body of the eldest Rogue brother.

"Um," I said, shocked that someone would speak so disdainfully at the first meeting.

The man gazed at me with sympathetic eyes before telling his companion to be quiet.

"I was just coming over to let Sarah and Jolee know that I was heading back to Haley's apartment."

Both of my friends jumped up from the couch at my admission, pulling themselves away from their boyfriends. Their eyes widened when they noticed how the crowd had grown in size. I envied that they could be so lost in their bubble and could hide away from the real world.

"Are you sure you have to go?" Jolee asked and I nodded, a headache beginning to form as I considered my options for finding a place to live before the school year started.

Sarah chimed in. "I feel really awful about the lease mix-up. You should come to stay with us until we can get it all resolved. It's my fault after all."

"It's okay, Sarah. I don't want to impose on you both. I'll figure something out, I'm sure."

After promising that I'd stay with either of them if I changed my mind, I moved to leave the party. Except when I opened the door, I ran smack dab into a hard chest.

"Oomph," I mumbled as I reached up and placed my hands on his taut chest, lingering a second too long as I felt the muscles tick beneath my palms. I also didn't fail to notice how good he smelled. It was some sort of mix between sandalwood and sweat.

"Watch where you're going, mouse."

Instantly I took a step back, only to bump into another person standing in the apartment's entryway and then the foot of a third.

"Sorry."

My apology fell on deaf ears as the trio sneered at me. My chin instantly fell to my chest, my dull brown hair curtaining my face. It was my defense mechanism—a way to shield me from the world and blend into the background.

Pushing past the group, I tumbled out into the hallway. I had resigned to myself that I wouldn't turn around and I would head straight to the apartment, but something called to me. Glancing over my shoulder I locked eyes with Chance, the gorgeous Ridge Rogue that I had bumped into. And he wasn't just gorgeous by normal standards; he was extraordinarily handsome. He had a jawline that could easily cut glass, lips that made a girl want to make an appointment with her local surgeon, dark hair that held the perfect amount of sinful waves as if he just finished fucking a girl in his bed, and eyes that were green orbs of emerald. It was those eyes that held me captive. They reminded me of something from my past. Memories that refused to surface, but the familiarity was there. Except as they narrowed, I suddenly wasn't sure if those memories were all good. He looked at me like I had crawled from the sewer and invaded his space.

Maybe I did.

With a yip I hurried to Haley's apartment. All of her furniture was still in place; the sublease offered the apartment furnished, so I was happy to have a bed to sleep in for the night. After that, I wasn't sure what I was going to do if the school couldn't find any open dorm rooms.

That was the downside of going to an exclusive private university and being in a small town about thirty minutes from Boston; there weren't a lot of options for living arrangements.

I took my time in the shower, knowing this could be the last one I'd get to take in a private space for a while. The stress of Sarah's mess-up weighed heavy. I felt anger deep in my gut that couldn't be acted upon. I knew that she had let the lease agreement slip through the cracks amidst her excitement to move in with Archer.

If I really wanted to get out of this mess, I knew I could simply contact my father. He had enough money to make everything right for me. But I refused to ask for his help. I wanted to experience college on my own terms. I had a part-time job with a local elementary school and a side project around campus that kept me busy. I conceded when he chose Wellington as the University out of the three choices that I would attend. He would pay my tuition, but I took care of everything else on my own.

It wasn't too long before the hot water ran out and I was forced to get out of the shower. Clad in only a towel, I went back to the room I was staying in and rummaged through my rolling suitcase. It held one pair of pajamas and about two weeks' worth of my clothes.

Snuggling under my blanket since the bed was bare from linens, I shut my eyes and tried to catch some sleep, but instead of dreamless slumber, I was haunted by the green eyes of Chance. It wasn't like this was my first time seeing him since Sarah and Jolee were dating his brothers, but usually, I tried to steer clear of any interaction. I was confident he had zero idea who I was. But the way he looked at me sent a chill down my spine, and not the good kind. The type of shiver you felt when you walked alone in the dark in an unfamiliar area. Yet, from everything I knew, Chance was a perfectly nice guy to those he allowed into his circle. And to those that shared his bed. The Ridge Rogues had a reputation after all.

Sighing, I reached for the delicate charm on the necklace that rested between my breasts. I'd had it as long as I could remember. Two tiny hearts interlocked and were woven through the thin gold chain. I'm not sure where I got it from, but I never took it off. Something deep inside me wouldn't allow it. I fiddled with the hearts as I tried to come up with a solution for my homelessness.

My anxiety mounted and I knew I wouldn't be able to sleep. Reaching for a small notebook and pen I stashed in my bag, I sat up in bed and opened the notebook to a blank page. At the top of the page, I listed a few options of where I could get some sleep, including asking a few of the teachers I worked with for a room and asking my father for help—neither option sounded great at the moment.

Then realizing that I had two more years left until I finished my degree, I started listing all of the things I wanted to do and experience before I began working for my father. It was sort of like a bucket list, but they were things most people would actually do in their lives. Items like dancing in the rain, going to a baseball game, and riding the subway made my top ten. My parents had kept me sheltered for most of my life, which was why my father had chosen such a private college.

I kept listing item after item until I heard the door to the apartment close. Glancing at my phone, I noticed two hours had passed since I returned to the apartment. Glancing down at the notebook I had scribbled my list on, I now had one hundred and fifty items listed in addition to my original three. Knowing I needed to get some sleep, I jotted one last item down and then set the notebook aside.

Closing my eyes, I was grateful to fall asleep finally.

None of my prospects for a living arrangement had panned out. I tried a women's shelter just outside of town, a few more friend's couches, a bench in the school courtyard (that one almost got me expelled when one of the campus officers found me), and the storage room in the school I worked at (which almost got me fired when they found me on the security cameras).

My time was running out with school starting in five days. Glancing around the large cafeteria, I watched from the corner as the newer students moved about without a care. They were all too engrossed in each other to notice the girl sitting in the corner with a suitcase, wondering what she would do next. I only had one option left at my disposal and I had to plan it just right.

The campus bell began to ring, signaling the nine o'clock evening hour. With a huff, I stood from my table and grabbed the handle of my suitcase. Staff began to shuffle about, wiping tables and sweeping, essentially shooing everyone from the space so that they could end their day.

Pulling the suitcase behind me, I left the confines of the cafeteria and stepped out onto the darkened pathway leading to the school courtyard.

There weren't enough lights around campus and I had mentioned it to the dean's receptionist more than once but was brushed off every time. Even when Jolee had been assaulted last year, they did little to remedy the problem. Apparently, the rich and elite preferred to lurk in the shadows.

My hands tightened around the strap of my purse, digging into the supple leather, while my other hand gripped the handle of my suitcase as I made my way toward the library. I knew it was open for a few more minutes as they began ushering students out. I had been studying the closing routine for the last week and knew that there was a slim window that would allow me to sneak past.

I slipped through the main entry in what I had hoped was stealth-like, but clumsy me tripped over my own feet in the process. Releasing the hold on my suitcase, my hands jutted forward, trying to catch myself before I took a nose dive into the marble floor. Pain radiated in my knees as they collided with the cold hard floor, the suitcase falling onto the back of my legs in the process.

A moment of silence passed as I tried to catch my breath, closing my eyes to seal out the world around me. Somewhere in the recesses of my mind, I heard a voice. It was rough and condescending, but not one that I recognized. I shook my head like a cartoon character that had stars circling around to clear my mind.

I counted to three and that was when I heard the first chuckle. My cheeks heated and I felt like a lobster tossed in boiling water. I was being served up on a platter for public consumption. One laugh turned into a dozen or so, the giggles echoing off the expansive foyer of the library. The small independent part of me wanted to turn around and stand with my head held high, and for a moment, I almost had, but my embarrassment got the better of me. I jumped up from the ground, grabbed my suitcase, and dove toward the side door that led to the stairwell.

I slammed my back against the door as it shut behind me and the wheels of my suitcase screeched against the concrete. If there were a horror film taking place, my heavy breathing would make me the main character.

"Are you okay?"

The question startled me and a yelp toppled from my lips as I stared up at the handsome face of the eldest Ridge Rogue. His shoulder-length hair was tied back and dark-framed glasses sat perched on his nose but did little to detract from his clear blue eyes. I knew from a rumor that Link was the graduate student whose class everyone signed up for. He was so popular that the dean had to put a limit on the number of enrollees.

"Are you?" he repeated, and speechlessly I nodded.

"Whatcha got there?" he asked as his chin pointed toward my suitcase.

Without a second thought, I shouted, "Books," then immediately cringed at how absurd that sounded.

"Books?"

"Yes. I. . .ugh. . .have a big project that I'm working on. It's just easier to carry them this way."

He gave me a skeptical glance. The kind where his eyes narrowed and one brow raised, causing his forehead to wrinkle slightly. I could tell he didn't believe me but was giving me the benefit of the doubt.

"Well, the library is closing up soon. Need help carrying that. . .thing back to your apartment?"

Gosh, I hated how nice he was. Here I was trying to find a decent place to sleep and he's trying to help me to my nonexistent car. Beads of sweat began to pool just along my hairline as the lies started to build.

"No!" I screeched, watching as his expression furrowed. "What I mean is, I left my notebook with all of my notes and study guides back at my table. I need to go grab it."

"Why don't I go. . ."

"No. Thank you, but I've got it. Thank you for your help."

Scooting around him, I dashed up the stairs as fast as I could with my suitcase knocking into my hip as I went. I said a silent prayer as I went knowing that at any moment the zipper could break apart and my lie would be strewn at my feet and Link's.

The third-floor landing came into view and I sighed in relief. Link was still waiting down at the bottom of the stairwell, but I dared not to peek over my shoulder.

With a firm grasp, I ripped the door open and found myself bathed in darkness, only a tiny flicker of red from the exit signs glowed in the space. Grabbing my phone from my back pocket, I turned on the flashlight app and made my way down the hall to the small room off the side. It was a space I occasionally came to when I needed peace and quiet. I knew that this was the least utilized area of the library, monitoring it closely for the last week, and I decided this was my destination for the next night or two.

In the shadows of the old, antique novels, I stashed my suitcase onto an open bottom shelf I discovered yesterday. Across the way, there was a secret cubby I revealed by accident yesterday when I was looking for a place to hide. I moved aside the heavy velvet curtain framing the windows on this level and found the small button. When I was snooping the day before, I noticed it when I was leaning against the side of the window, trying to figure out my next move. A few grad students were milling about, so I couldn't press it then.

With my fingers crossed, I pressed it and closed my eyes, hoping that I hadn't set off something catastrophic. Luckily I risked a quick peep, just a smidge, only to widen both eyes in surprise. I came face to face with a pocket-sized room built into the wall. There was a small desk with a lamp in the space and that was it. I reached out to flick it on but the bulb had long since burned out. Its setup reminded me of the dark rooms used to keep daylight from harming old paper.

The room itself was just big enough for me to lay down if I positioned myself just right. Grabbing the blanket and inflatable pillow shoved at the top of my suitcase, I created a makeshift bunker for the night in the dusty niche. Locating the button that would shut the door, I pressed it quickly, praying that I wouldn't end up locked inside and made myself as comfortable as the concrete floor would allow.

Luck was on my side when I found this room. I knew how to curl my body into a small enough size so that I could be overlooked. Otherwise, I was prepared to sleep between the dusty stacks on the floor.

I just hoped that I'd find a place to live sooner rather than later because I wasn't sure that my current arrangement was going to last very long.

RENEE HARLESS

CHAPTER TWO

CHANCE

My senior year was going about as splendidly as I imagined it would. The early morning baseball practice had only exasperated the hangover I had woken with. Tossing the wet towel onto the bench in the locker room, I tugged on my boxers then went to search for an aspirin.

I had zero desire to continue playing, but it was the reason for my scholarship. And I was determined to keep Tracy, my mother, from shelling out a dime toward my education. Luckily, most of my tuition was free because she was a professor at the university, but all of my other expenses were covered by skills playing baseball.

It also helped that my youngest brother, Tyler, had joined the team this year.

"Good practice," he shouted from beside me. I flinched involuntarily as it rang in my ear like an off-pitch flute.

"Geez. Rough night?"

"Rough morning," I replied as I finished pulling on the rest of my clothes, remembering how the girl from last night was more than eager to spend countless hours having me pound into her pussy. It wasn't until the alarm on my phone sounded that I knew I had made a drunken mistake. Baseball practice on no sleep and the taste of bourbon still on my tongue was not the best way to start the day. Nor was remembering her vicious glare when I had to kick her out of my apartment. Not that I ever had a repeat performance with the women I took to bed. I left before they could even consider digging their claws deep into my skin. I was already regretting my mistake of bringing her back to my place to begin with. I usually had one of my brothers to deal with, but Rylan had left to study overseas for the semester, leaving me a quiet place for once.

"Aw, did pretty boy not get his beauty sleep?" Tyler teased as he slipped his towel from his shoulders and did his own quick change.

If only he knew the things I did between the sheets – pretty wouldn't be the word he would describe. I preferred things rough and dirty, usually to keep the woman I was with too occupied with the sensations to pay attention to anything other than her pleasure.

Brushing off Tyler's comment, I ran my hand through my wet hair and grabbed my gym bag from my locker. "Will I see you at mom's house on Sunday?" I asked him. Our adoptive mom, Tracy, was a stickler about Sunday dinners at her house. It was a tradition since the eldest brother Link enrolled at Wellington. My brothers had our own version on Friday nights, though the size of the gatherings had started to outgrow our spaces.

"Yeah, mom wants to see my schedule for the semester."

I didn't have to look at Tyler to know that he was rolling his eyes. As the baby, he hated when mom treated him like he couldn't do anything without her help. Too bad he seemed to have forgotten that we all went through the same nagging when we enrolled in the university.

"Just do it as we all did. You know how excited she is to have all of us staying here. At least you're no longer living under her roof."

"I guess," he said with a huff; the sound of his locker closing echoed in the locker room.

"See ya later," I called out as I headed from the locker room, hoping that the coach didn't call for me as I passed his office. I wasn't his favorite player, not because of any shenanigans on the field, but by the things that happened off the field. I had more than one woman toss my name through the mud to get my attention after a night that she couldn't forget.

The fog hung heavy in the air as I walked back from the field house. The summer in New England began to give way to fall. Sometimes I forgot that Wellington University was only thirty minutes outside of Boston in the small town of Wellington. The town was the college except for a small downtown that took up residence on three blocks of Main Street. Tracy liked to say that we lived in our own *Hallmark* town.

The campus was deserted as I strolled across the quad. Most students wouldn't be waking up for another few hours, at least until classes started up next week. As I passed the main dining hall, my stomach let out a growl loud enough to rival the crowd at the World

Series. It seemed that my body wanted food over a few hours of rest.

My brothers and I were more inclined to cook our meals; something Tracy ingrained in us when we joined her family as teens. Venturing on campus for a bite to eat was definitely going to be a downgrade, but it would suffice for the morning. If I had my way, I would head to the diner just off campus for a greasy breakfast; too bad my stomach was guiding me at the moment.

Surprise registered when I entered the large cafeteria and found more than a few people milling about. Most looked like freshmen trying to scrape together a meal without their parents' assistance for the first time, while others seemed like graduate students already neck-deep in class work. In the corner, I noticed a handful of black-suited men doing their best to be inconspicuous but doing an awful job at it. The school must be catering to a few upper-crust students this year.

Grabbing two biscuits and a bottle of water, I made my way to a table against a set of windows and looked out into the cafeteria. I made it a rule never to have my back facing the crowd. Having someone sneak up on me was not an experience I wanted to partake in again.

Memories began flooding my mind, blocking my view of my surroundings. Images of burners, tubing, and fire flicked back and forth like a movie. I could still hear the sound of sirens as the backdrop to the visions.

Squeezing my eyes shut, I willed the visions away until finally it went black. Slamming my fists on the table as I opened my eyes, the pain reverberated through my knuckles, but I felt nothing—my anger at the images surfacing bubbled out of control.

The sound of my pummeling against the particleboard and plastic startled the girl passing in front of me. She screeched and froze in place. Her eyes grew twice their size as if she had come face to face with a monster. She had no idea how close she was to one.

"What?" I growled, the bellow vibrating deep in my chest. As expected, she jumped and scurried away, a suitcase trailing behind her as she went. It was odd, but I had witnessed stranger things since enrolling in college.

I finished the two biscuits, ignoring the stares the students were trying not so hard to hide. Chugging the water, I wiped the back of my hand against my mouth and stood from the table. A few diners winced as the chair screeched loudly against the floor.

Mumbling under my breath I walked toward the trash can to throw away the wrapper and water bottle. Out of the corner of my eye, I noticed that the girl I had scared earlier was scribbling wildly in a notebook. She looked familiar. I'd seen her around campus before, but it was something more than that and I couldn't put my finger on it.

She must have felt my stare. Slamming the notebook closed, she gripped it in her hands and held it toward her chest, all while placing her gaze everywhere but on me. She reminded me of a trapped animal—a little mouse.

Recognition dawned on me that she was the girl that had stumbled out of my apartment when we threw Rylan a going away party. That must be why I knew she looked familiar.

Back at my apartment, I fell back in bed wanting to savor my last Friday before school started. I'd need to find someone who could ensure I kept a good grade in my classes while playing ball. Usually, I could convince one of the younger classmen to help by getting them tickets to games to impress girls. Hopefully, I'd find someone this year, or the dean would assign someone to me. He made the mistake of trusting a female graduate student my freshman year. It only took two study sessions before she caved to my advances. I hadn't seen her on campus since then. Rumor was that she transferred to another university after I told her it was a one-time thing.

It was midday when I finally pulled myself out of dreamland – a place I hated. Dreams usually meant memories that refused to stay locked away. More tired than I had been before I laid my head on the pillow, I shuffled to my kitchen and put together a couple of sandwiches before sprawling on the couch. Flipping through the channels, I landed on a cooking show that pitted a well-known chef celebrity against an unknown. Cooking was one of my favorite hobbies though I rarely had the time to work on it.

Losing myself in the show's marathon, I thought about all of the things I could do this semester without a roommate. Truthfully it was the first time that I'd be alone since I was a kid.

My gut clenched as I thought about my childhood, the snippets of what I could remember flickering into place like puzzle pieces.

"No, no, NO!" I shouted as I leaned forward, resting my elbows on my knees and my head between my hands. My fingers gripped at my hair as I tried to snap out of it. I needed to break free.

Launching myself from the couch, I practically sprinted as I grabbed my keys and dove out of my apartment, taking the stairs down to the first level two or three at a time.

Air. I needed air. The building was suffocating me; the walls felt like they were squeezing my lungs like a vice.

I heaved oxygen into my chest, the muscles burning with each gasp. I'd almost drowned once, at the hands of someone that was supposed to take care of me, and it felt like that. It burned like that.

I rested my hands on my knees, hunched over until I could get my bearings about me. Time was a blur as I focused on bringing each breath of air and filling my lungs. When I finally got my wits about me, I stood to my full six-foot four frame and looked at the grassy area just beyond the entrance to the apartment complex.

Out of the corner of my eye I noticed a group of guys, probably freshmen, staring at me as if they'd just witnessed a monster escape from its cage. It's the closest depiction of what I kept tightly packed inside my skin. I was bred to be a monster that everyone feared. And they should. My family made sure of that.

Narrowing my eyes in their direction, I shouted, "See something interesting?" Wordlessly they scattered away like little cockroaches in the light.

Running my hands through my hair as I watch their retreating backs, my eyes landed on the girl from earlier in the cafeteria. She shuffled across the open area with a large group trailing on her heels. The group looked younger, like middle school age, and with various disabilities that I could see from a distance.

I wondered if she was giving a tour of some sort when I heard my name called out in the opposite direction; I turned to find a woman in a short red mini dress hobbling toward me wearing a pair of heels. She looked like she was ready for a night of clubbing and not lunch, as I assumed was the time based on the sun.

The girl from earlier forgotten, I tucked my hands into my pockets and waited for Magnolia to make her way over to me. She was a clinger in the first degree, not just because I was a baseball player for the school, but because I was a Ridge Rogue, the name given to my brothers and me because we were the ones everyone at the university wanted. They either wanted in our bed or wanted to be us. We never asked for the moniker, but one of Link's scorned lovers bestowed it upon us, and the name stuck.

"There's my favorite Ridge Rogue," she purred as she approached, wrapping her arms around my neck as I stood there unmoving.

"Is that what you told Rylan before he left?" I bellowed. She had nabbed two of us brothers before we found out that she had plans to add each of us to her bedpost. Not that we didn't get around, but fucking someone that had been with a brother was against our rules.

"Oh, Chance. You know that was a one-time thing. A mistake, really. You know that you're the rogue for me."

Reaching up, I untangled her arms from around my neck and held them to her sides with a tight grasp on her wrists. "You need to leave, Magnolia. I told you then that it was a one-time thing, yet you still come around every couple of weeks hoping for round two. It's not going to happen."

"But, Chance," she whimpered and I fought against the need to cringe at her nasally tone.

"But nothing. Go away, Magnolia."

Releasing her wrists with a slight shove, I stepped back from the red-sheathed dragon that wanted to dig her claws into me as I dismissed her offer.

"You're going to regret this. My daddy can destroy you."

"Great," I told her as I glanced over my shoulder, "I look forward to it."

Stepping back inside the complex, I let the glass door close behind me with my name echoing in the small lobby from Magnolia's shouts. Should I be worried that she will have her mafia king father destroy any life plans I have for the future? Probably, but I wasn't worried about the future. I barely woke up concerned about the present. It was the past that left its mark.

"Pass the butter, Oscar the grouch," someone called out from the other end of the table. We were sitting at the table in Link and Tyler's apartment. Suddenly I felt a roll collide with my forehead and my gaze bounced up from my plate to the person across from me, Jolee, who immediately pointed toward her boyfriend Ford, who was sitting right next to her.

"What?" I growled at him.

"I asked you to pass the butter. What has you all angry? Your face is pinched more than usual."

Not replying, I passed the butter across the table and turned my attention back to my plate of steak and vegetables. Conversation flowed around me, but I ignored it all until Jolee's worried voice carried across to my ears.

"What do you mean she hasn't told you where she's living?" she forcefully whispered to her friend Sarah who was sitting next to me and her boyfriend Archer. Jolee probably thought she was being quiet, but anyone at the table would have to be deaf not to hear the question. Ford always liked to joke that she didn't have an indoor voice.

"I don't know. I keep asking her and she deflects, then she's started to ignore my phone calls. I know she's not at the school or found an apartment because I've been watching the housing portal every day and nothing has opened up. I tried to follow her the other day and she just disappears. It's like she knows that I know something is up."

"Well, I'm sure she's fine. It's been two weeks. Maybe she asked her dad to put her up somewhere."

Leaning forward, Sarah placed both her hands on the sides of her plate as she said, "You know that calling her dad is the last thing that she wants to do."

"Maybe we can track her down, trace her number or something."

"If she'd ever answer her phone, that would be a good plan."

From the far side of the table, the sound of a drinking glass slamming drew our attention to Link. How the glass didn't shatter in his hand was beyond me.

"I'll take care of it," he growled, leaving everyone at the table speechless.

Everyone except me because I never knew when to shut my mouth.

"Maybe she doesn't want any of you to bother her. Ever think of that? And really, what kind of friends are you that you've pretty much abandoned someone and left her homeless. Now, what's for dessert?" I didn't care what kind of sweets there would be. I was more interested in heading downtown and finding a scantily-clad treat to lose myself in for the next twelve hours.

CHAPTER THREE

KEELEY

It was four days before school was slated to start and I had come no closer to finding a place to live than I had been two weeks ago. Thank goodness my academic advisor emailed me my schedule when my mail was returned to his office. I also knew that I had one more day to fix my living situation or I would have to suck it up and call my father, which was the last thing that I wanted to do. Living under his thumb my entire childhood, I had hoped for at least four years of freedom. That had already been cut short by one year when I went to a local community college against my father's wishes. If I accepted his help now, I would be one step closer to losing all of my freedom.

The alarm on my phone sounded – 4a.m. If I wanted to grab a shower and get ready for the day before anyone noticed my whereabouts, I needed to head to the gym on campus before five. As I sat up in the wall cubby, I unlocked my phone's screen and found two messages from my ex-boyfriend Thomas. He wanted to let me know that he was back on campus and wanted to see if we could meet up. I wasn't interested. He and I had little chemistry and he was a notorious flirt, something I did not tolerate.

Leaving the messages unread, I grabbed my things from the floor and shoved them back into my suitcase. I had gone through all of the clothes that I could fit and I desperately needed to find a cheap laundromat. Thank goodness I was still getting a paycheck for my part-time work with the local school system. I was an office assistant that spent most of my time helping out in the special education classes. If I had a choice, that would be the career path I'd pursue, but unfortunately, my future was already decided for me.

It took about ten minutes for me to gather all of my belongings and make the trek down to the first floor, doing my best not to set off any alarms. I had done that the first night and I was certain that the security guard would find me and kick me out. Luckily, he never even made it to my floor and I knew from that moment on that there would be no late-night bathroom trips.

Lugging my suitcase behind me, I press the horizontal bar for one of the side doors to the library and step out into the darkened landing. Every morning I said to myself that the school needed to invest in more lighting, especially with the money they were bringing in from the families of my elite classman.

Just as I made my way down the two steps, struggling to keep a hold of my suitcase, I ran into a brick wall, the kind of brick wall with a taut body and detailed muscles that I could feel beneath my pressed cheek.

"Oh no," I mumbled under my breath, sure that one of the few campus cops had been waiting for me to make my appearance.

"What is it with you and your friends always needing my help?" he asked in a deep voice that caused me to jump and look him in the face. He was no cop. I was confident that even in the darkness of early morning, I was looking at the head Ridge Rogue, Link.

"What. . .?" I began to ask as I pushed away from his body, both palms of my hands pressed against his chest.

"You're coming with me," he demanded as he reached down and grabbed the strap of my suitcase and lifted it from the ground. He didn't even bother to use the rolling handle.

Link took large strides, and it took me double the amount of steps to catch up with him. "Where are we going? I'm not going somewhere with you!"

I tried to reach for the strap on the side of the luggage, but he quickly moved it out of my reach, anticipating my action.

"I'm pretty certain that you don't have a choice or should I tell the school that you currently have no living arrangements, which would mean you're booted from the school. Or I could call your father." That had me catching my breath. He was throwing real threats in my direction and I didn't know why.

"No. . .no," I stuttered, my steps faltering as I continued to follow him. We continued the trek across campus until we approached a familiar apartment.

"Link," I said hesitantly as he walked through the front door with my suitcase, not even bothering to hold it open for me. I called his name out again and again, my voice growing louder with each flight of stairs.

"Link, I'm not staying with you!"

"That's not the plan," he said as he pulled out a key and quickly opened the door to an apartment as I made my way to the landing. I recognized the door and before I could argue again, Link clutched my elbow and dragged me inside.

"This is where you'll stay for at least the semester. It's perfectly safe and you'll have your own room."

"I can't afford. . ." I disputed, knowing that one of these apartments rented for more than I made with my part-time work.

"It's taken care of. Don't argue anymore, Keeley," he said as he practically tossed me onto the leather couch.

"Who put you up to this? Was it Sarah or Jolee?"

Completely ignoring me, he gave me the kind of look that had you immediately shutting your mouth. It was one that I was very familiar with; my father used it quite frequently. There was no use in arguing further.

"Chance," he called out as he leaned against the wall opposite of where I sat, his eyes pinned to me, making sure I didn't move a muscle. I couldn't even if I tried. Terrified out of my mind was what kept me trapped in place.

"Chance!" he shouted more forcefully, his deep voice echoing in the apartment. I jolted where I sat.

"What the fuck, man? It's four in the morning," a voice heavy with sleep grew louder as it approached.

"Damn, Chance. Put on some fucking pants," Link said, and despite my desire to hide away in a corner, I turned my head and stared at the man standing buck naked where the hall met the living room. His arms were crossed against his chest as he stood confidently in front of his brother.

And was that a silver ball glimmering on his pe. . .

My thoughts were interrupted as Chance threw his arms down and shouted something in Link's face. They must have continued their conversation as I ogled his pierced cock. I hadn't seen many in my young years, but Chance was quite well-endowed, from what I could tell.

"Give him a second to cool down." I turned my attention to Link and found him with a cocky smirk directed at me. My cheeks heated knowing that he caught me perusing his brother. Not that I could help it; he had been walking around naked.

"I really think I should leave," I repeated as I stood up from the couch and wiped my sweaty palms against my athletic pants.

"Sit," he growled, his smile quickly forgotten. I immediately sat back in place.

It only took a minute before Chance graced us with his presence, walking back out with a pair of gray sweatpants hanging loosely on his hips. He probably had no idea how good he looked in those pants. I almost thought they were better than seeing him naked. Almost.

"Get your fill, mouse?" He sneered at me and I realized once again that I had been gawking at him unabashedly.

"Sorry," I murmured as I turned my eyes back to my knees, bouncing wildly in place.

"Maybe you can call me later tonight for a repeat?" a sultry voice purred, but I was too wary of turning around again. I was certain that it was a beautiful woman that had the perfect just fucked look as she left Chance's bed.

"Not going to happen. I told you the rules last night."

"Are you telling me that you don't want any of this again? Don't you remember that thing I did with my legs?"

That left me wondering. I wasn't very flexible, so I could only imagine the limber body the voice must have possessed.

"Get out. Now."

He was so incredibly harsh and cold it left me perplexed at how he seemed to have a revolving door of women. All of the Ridge Rogues did, at least until Ford and Archer had been tamed by my friends.

I didn't hear her reply, but I jumped in place as the apartment door slammed.

"Keep better company, Chance," Link's fatherly voice rang out.

"Stay the fuck out of my business. Now, remind me again, why the hell are you here at this ungodly hour? It's my only day free from practice."

"Keeley is going to live here for a while."

"Who the hell is Keeley? And what kind of name is that?"

Jumping from my perch on the sofa, I stood and turned to both men. "I'm right here. Stop talking like I'm invisible. And Keeley is a family name."

Chance immediately looked at his brother and took a menacing step toward him while pointing at me. "She is not staying here. No."

"Yes, she is." Link crossed his arms as if his word was the final say.

"No, she's not."

"I really don't want to."

"Look, neither of you have a choice. Rylan's rent is paid up and she needs a place to live to stay in school. I'm sure you two won't even see each other. Come on, Chance, you know this is what mom would want."

"Dammit," Chance said as he waved a hand through his wavy tresses. "For how long?" he asked as he turned his stare toward me.

"A semester. Just until Haley comes back or I can find another place to live."

He seemed to contemplate my answer, his eyes narrowing as he skimmed my body. I was wearing an oversized sweatshirt that hung down to my knees and black athletic pants with my worn tennis shoes. To anyone else I looked like a bum off the streets, not the kid of a multimillion-dollar CEO.

"Fine. Just stay out of my way. Where's your stuff?"

"This is it," Link pointed out, and I did nothing to add that I had all of my things in storage. I was currently shelling out money for the unit so I could grab my things as I needed them. Maybe Jolee would let me borrow Ford's car or something or I could ask one of the teachers that I worked with. Thomas had a small luxury SUV, but I had zero desire to reach out to him to borrow it.

Without a word, Link carried my luggage down the hall, I assumed to a second bedroom.

"Look, Keeley," Chance said, his lips sneering at he said my name. "There is only one bathroom. I don't want your girly shit all over the place. I have practice every day but Saturday at five in the morning and again in the afternoon. When I'm not here, the television is yours, but when I am, I get control," he explained. I noticed how he emphasized the word control as if he had to keep control of all things in his life.

"I won't be a problem. I spend most of my time at the library or in my room. You won't even know that I'm here."

"I doubt that," he murmured.

"And don't worry about any lady friends you bring over. I have some noise-canceling headphones that work great," I said, rambling. I did that when I was nervous and the way Chance's scowl continued to deepen as I spoke plucked my nerves until I was shaking in place. My fingers twisted with each other as I brought my hands together in front of my hips. I could no longer look him in the eye, opting to avert my gaze to his neck instead.

"Thank you for. . .um. . .letting me crash. I promise I won't be a burden."

"Doesn't seem like I had much of a choice. Link tends to take on charity cases and we just have to go along for the ride until they've used up all of his kindness."

Pulling my gaze from his neck, I locked eyes with him, furious that he would assume I was using his brother. "I am not a charity case. I didn't ask to be helped. He threatened me, quite frankly."

"Good to see you have a little fire in you, mouse. I'm going to the gym. I'll be back in the next hour. Link can give you his key since I'm sure he has hundreds of copies."

His hostility toward me was overwhelming, it left my heart thumping wildly in my chest to where the only reaction I could muster was to fight back. Flight wasn't an option for me. He had no reason to hate me, and I would have assumed since his brother's dated my friends that he would at least extend an olive branch of niceties, but he acted if I was no better than a piece of gum he'd stepped in wearing his favorite pair of shoes.

It seemed this living situation was going to be a jarring experience. Hopefully I could change his mind about me before we ripped each other's heads off. The forced proximity wasn't ideal for me either.

Grabbing a bag next to the entry door, Chance hefted it onto his shoulder, still shirtless, and made his exit. Link joined me a second later and explained about the laundry room downstairs and how he and his brothers have family dinner night every Friday at one of their apartments. They also had a family dinner at their mother's house on Sundays. I guessed that meant I needed to make myself scarce on the night's dinner was hosted at Chance's apartment.

After setting his extra key on the counter, Link left me alone in the apartment. How did he know that I wasn't a kleptomaniac or a stalker that planned to ransack the place?

Timidly I walked out of the living room and down the hall, my arms wrapped around myself as a protective mechanism. I found two doors directly across from each other. Opening the door on the left, I was startled as the hinges squeaked at the movement. Instead of a bedroom, I looked inside a surprisingly clean bathroom. Like, far cleaner than any I had seen from any college student. It made me wonder if Chance was a neat freak or if he hired someone to clean the apartment. I was a tidy person by nature, organization being something that kept my mind from getting scrambled on a day-to-day basis.

The bathroom was a mix of whites and cream with classic white and black hexagon penny tiles on the floor. The bathtub was larger than I would have thought for a college apartment and I was instantly in love. I wondered if Chance would be okay with me using it every now and then. Probably not. It seemed like he didn't even want to remember that I was underfoot.

I made a mental note to figure out how much I needed to give him for rent and utilities. Despite Link claiming that everything was covered, I wanted to take care of my share of expenses. I wasn't a freeloader and I didn't want to owe anyone anything.

Stepping out of the bathroom, I turned around and opened the other door across the way. I gasped as it creaked. The room was massive. I expected a twin bed, maybe a full-sized, a dresser and possibly enough room for a desk or bookshelf. Boy, was I glad to be wrong. There was a king-size bed with a black duvet that would be replaced once I had a chance to get to my storage unit or a store. Two dressers flanked a single window across from a full-length closet. Across from the bed, there was an empty desk with a bookshelf to the left. Honestly, the room was perfect for me.

I'd have thought it was the main bedroom if my suitcase wasn't sitting on the floor beside the bed, the top unzipped. I cringed thinking that Link had sifted through my things, but I was so far out of my element I couldn't even bother to be embarrassed.

Knowing that I would only get to spend a semester or so in the space broke my heart a little. Under any other circumstances I would beg Chance to let me stay, but that was never going to happen. I planned to stay as invisible as possible.

The teeth of the zipper snapped together as I tugged up the slider on the suitcase. I grabbed my purse and the key Link left on the counter with my other hand while the suitcase trailed behind me, and made my way down the stairs to the laundry room. I was thankful that it was empty when I arrived. Not bothering to sort through everything, I tossed all of my laundry into the industrial-sized top-load washer and fed it detergent and my money.

Now, I just had to figure out what I could do to decorate the room without setting off my temporary roommate.

As I made the journey up the stairs, I received a new group text from Jolee and Sarah asking if I wanted to meet up with them for brunch. I hesitated at my response. I knew they were going to ask of my whereabouts and I wasn't sure I was at liberty to tell them, but lying to my friends wasn't something I could do. After living with Sarah for a year, she knew me better than anyone.

I trudged back inside the apartment after dealing with Link's key, which stuck in the lock and took me five solid minutes to remove and try again. I didn't know how he was able to open it so quickly earlier.

Deciding to utilize the shower while it was free, I hopped under the hot spray and washed off with a generic body wash that I kept for my showers at the gym. I'd never cleansed myself so quickly, a new record I was sure, then realized that I had nothing to dry off with. I hated stepping out of the shower without a towel, but it was in the wash downstairs. Dripping water on the tile floor, I opened the bathroom door a tad and I listened for any signs that Chance had returned. Finding the apartment empty, I gathered the clothes from earlier and made a mad dash across the hall to my temporary room.

Ignoring my friend's messages on my phone like a horrible human being, I got to work tugging out my notebook and few electronics like my laptop and placing them on the desk. Glancing at the time and noticing that I still had about five minutes before I needed to switch out my laundry to the dryer, I opened up my journal and added a few more items to my college bucket list. Remembering the piercing on Chance's dick, I added a hidden piercing to my list. I knew nothing about that form of body modification, only having my earlobes done, but it seemed like something my dad would never know.

Rushing downstairs to switch out my laundry, I returned to the apartment and noticed the unlocked door. I began freaking out, thinking that I had left the lock unlatched and a burglar had walked into the space or the crazy woman from this morning had returned. I heard movement in the kitchen and grabbed the closest thing to the door, a baseball bat resting in the corner.

In my hand, I gripped the smooth wood and rested the end on my shoulder as I slowly approached the kitchen counter peninsula. The lights were still off in the apartment and the blinds closed from the small sliding glass doors, but there was enough light for me to see that a man was hunched over in what appeared to be a pantry.

"Ah!!!!" I screamed as I charged forward, bat raised above my head as my weapon. Like a Viking warrior of the past, I was destined to defend the apartment from the intruder. Chance turned around, grabbed the bat in his strong grip and lifted me in the air.

"What the fuck is your problem, mouse?"

"I. . .I. . .I,"

"Out with it," he growled as he brought me closer to him, my toes scraping against the wooden vinyl floors during the journey.

"I thought someone had broken in."

"And you didn't happen to think that it was, you know, the person that rents the apartment?"

"No. . .I wasn't thinking that. I just knew that I locked the door but then questioned myself."

Despite the anger radiating from him, I couldn't help myself from staring into his eyes. They were a warm mossy green that I could easily lose myself in. I needed to remind myself that Chance was not a man that wanted more than one night. Or would give someone as homely as me a second glance.

"Stop looking at me like that," he growled, bringing me another inch closer.

Something in me changed, an inner light flickered on, and a side of me that rarely made itself present emerged. It was the side of me that always got me in trouble growing up. My father, teachers, and classmates always said I had a mouth on me. But what they rarely added was that I didn't have a mouth until I was instigated, then a red-eyed monster emerged from deep inside.

Yanking myself and the bat free from his grasp with a few shakes of my hips, I glared up at him as if he was a professor that gave me a failing grade. How dare he.

"Look, mister," I began with a shove of the bat's end into his chest, "I was trying to protect your apartment, which you so reluctantly allowed me to stay in. So, excuse me if I was trying to help you out. I didn't expect you home yet."

An awkward pause passed between us, and I almost removed the end of the bat from his chest, but didn't want to lose the upper hand.

"Are you done poking me now?" he asked, his expression never changing from the scowl he wore since I arrived this morning.

Biting my lip, I replied, "Um. . .yes?"

"Just remember, little mouse, this is my place and I'm only letting you stay here because I have the room. Next time you think there is a threat, just turn around and walk away. It will end up better for you."

He moved around me effortlessly, like a skater on the ice, leaving me standing in his wake, then my fury simmered close to the surface.

"I'm not some fragile thing, you know. I could have taken you out if you were a robber."

"Sure, that's about as likely a scenario as I am to have a repeat performance with the woman from this morning. And tell me, little mouse, did you like what you saw?" he added with a laugh as he made his way down the hall until he disappeared into his bedroom.

"Grrr," I vocalized as I placed the bat back in the corner at the entrance and stomped back to what would be my bedroom.

I hoped that an apartment would open up on the student portal sometime soon because I wasn't sure that I could handle this.

RENEE HARLESS

CHAPTER FOUR

CHANCE

She hadn't annoyed me as much as I had expected - the little mouse living in my apartment. I assumed that I would have had to call an exterminator by the end of day two, but she had kept herself tucked inside her room, only coming out for a few meals where she ignored my grunts.

Should I have been nicer to her? Probably. But I couldn't explain the way she left my body on edge whenever she was close. There was something about her that made me want to tell her all of my secrets, but I couldn't risk that. Instead, I fought her anytime we were together. It was the only way I could keep her and others at a safe distance. There were no other options.

Something about her left me on edge. I wasn't sure if it was from Link threatening me to have her stay or the fact that my dreams had returned with a vengeance. Usually, I could go a day or two without memories making themselves known, easily able to push them away with some sort of extracurricular activity. But no matter what I did, even the long hours at the gym, I found that they returned no matter what.

I was getting tired of it.

Luckily, tonight was dinner with mom and she was making my favorite stuffed shells. I hoped to head over there a bit earlier to help her prepare the meal. Cooking was something that brought me a bit of joy, though I never let any of my brothers in on that secret. Tracy was the only one who knew. It was something she stumbled upon when I was up late one night in high school, toying around with some ingredients in her spaghetti sauce. She had asked if I wanted to learn and I allowed her to show me a few tricks. My past wasn't brought up then, and I hoped it would stay that way.

Too bad my memories weren't getting the memo.

"I'll be back later," her soft voice said as if she was wary and planning for an attack. I supposed she wasn't too far off base, but every time I opened my mouth to speak to her, something vile came spewing out. I wasn't sure why, but I couldn't control it. I was a volcano sitting dormant until Keeley, and I exploded around her.

"Yeah, sure," I murmured as I stood from the couch and made my way to the bathroom, waiting to hear the door close.

Finishing up, I stepped out of the bathroom and peered across the way to the room where Keeley was staying. I hadn't cared how she decorated or what she kept in the space, but curiosity got the better of me.

I took the two steps across the way and opened her door, half expecting a bucket of water or blood to pour on my head. After the bat incident, it seemed like something that she would do. Glancing around the space, I was surprised to see Rylan's once dark room transformed into a feminine retreat. The bed was covered in peach, pink, and cream-colored blankets with two pillows too many. The dresser had pictures strategically placed on the top, but I ignored them and focused on the desk where one large picture sat. It seemed to be from her high school graduation. Keeley was wearing a white cap and gown next to a set of people that she didn't resemble to my naked eye, but I was too focused on her expression. She looked like she wanted to be anywhere else.

Pulling my eyes away from the frame, I looked down at the open notebook, and a Grinch-like grin pulled across my lips. Keeley had written in girly-swirled letters: Bucket List.

Grabbing the spiral book, I took it from her desk and carried it back to my room, perusing the list as I went. She had off the wall things noted with stars: a tattoo, a hidden piercing (whatever that was), learn self-defense, and cook a meal. She had a list of things most people accomplished by the time they entered college.

For split second I'd wondered if Keeley was sick or something, but then immediately tossed that aside. All I knew was that I had some fun ammunition with which to tease her.

Throwing the book on my bed, I laid back and stared up at the ceiling. My phone buzzed on the nightstand and I glanced over to find another woman calling, another in a long line of empty nights. Sometimes I wondered why so many people at the university put us on a pedestal. Besides my brothers and me being good-looking guys, we were assholes to pretty much everyone, including professors, but for some reason, people seemed to find it a trait they could overlook. It even stumped me most days.

I wasn't sure how long I laid staring at the ceiling fan, but I heard the door unlock. Keeley's voice resonated around the apartment and I realized that she was on the phone. I sat up in bed, not trying to eavesdrop, but I couldn't help myself.

"Yes, sir," she said in a tone that seemed a bit sad if you asked me.

"No, sir. It was just a mix-up with the school. If I finish my course work this year, I could graduate early next year, but it would push it to finish this year. I'm not sure the school will allow me to take that many credit hours at once. Are you sure that you want me to take over the business? Isn't Damon a better fit?"

Her father sounded like a dick from the one-sided conversation I was listening to, but who was I to judge what someone did with their life? Hell, I didn't even know what I planned to do when I graduated. Maybe go to culinary school if I wasn't drafted, which I seriously doubted.

She continued to speak with her father, and by the way her voice trailed off, I could tell that she had made her way back to her bedroom. Sparkly notebook in hand, I decided to start round one of torment Keeley.

I waited for her to finish her phone call before making her aware of my presence. Leaning against the jamb of her door, I crossed my arms against my chest with her notebook tucked protectively between my hands.

Deep in my chest a laugh began to bubble up, and I had to fight to push it down as her back stiffened while placing her phone on the now empty desk.

"What's the matter, Keeley? Missing something?"

"No. . .I. . ." she said with hunched shoulders as she slowly turned to face me.

"Are you sure?" I asked as I pushed away from the door and stepped closer to her with the notebook opened. "I found this amazing book with a bucket list of sorts."

"Give it back!" she said as she lunged for it, only for my height to thwart her attempt as I held the notebook above her head.

"No. I think I'll hang onto it a bit longer."

"Chance, please. You shouldn't have gone through my things. It's a violation!"

Shrugging my shoulders, I simply replied, "My apartment."

"God, don't be such an asshole and just give it back."

"But I like being an asshole, it brings out this fiery side in you, little mouse."

"Gah!" she exclaimed as she jumped for the notebook again, only for her fingertips to scrape the bottom of the book barely. "What do you even want it for?"

"I don't know. Light reading? Maybe I'll give it back when I'm done."

"You know what?" she stated with her hands in fists resting at her hips. She looked like a deranged Wonder Woman. "Keep it. I don't care. I have other things to do. Important things. Things that matter. Unlike you who seems to have nothing better to do than bed every woman you come in contact with."

"Everyone but you," I chimed in. "I don't do users."

"User? Excuse me?"

"Yeah. Used my brother for his hospitality, used your father for a job, I'm sure the list goes on and on."

"I didn't. . .you know what? I don't need to explain myself to you. If you don't mind, I have a project to work on, and then I have dinner plans. Please get out. I'll have some sort of rent for you by the end of the day. Maybe that will keep you from going through my things."

The tips of my fingernails dug into the roughened skin of my palms as I clenched my fists. Something about Keeley's words triggered a recollection, a memory that had been safely tucked away in a locked box. It was from a past event, the time when my world was flipped upside down, and I was forced to be someone else. I had been five someone else's since I was born.

I clenched my eyes shut as I stood in her doorway, praying for the blackness to wash away the images of bags, toys, and clothes. I couldn't figure out why it seemed so familiar.

A soft hand pressed against my bare forearm and I jerked back like she had scalded me with a branding iron.

"Are you okay? You look sick?"

"Don't fucking touch me," I seethed, unable to pull myself from the grip of the false reality I had found myself in. "You don't get to lay a hand on me, mouse. I'll leave your shit alone when I feel like it."

She crossed her arms and stood toe to toe against me. If I weren't so fucked in my own head, I'd probably take a moment to realize that she was quite attractive when she was fired up with her pink cheeks and narrowed gaze.

"Fine, then it seems like that gives me permission to go through yours. Make sure you don't have any skeletons in that closet, Chance, because I'm going to find them all."

Stepping back, I tossed the book inside her room, the thick covers landing with a bounce on her bed. Leaning down, the tip of my nose pressed against hers as I said, "No skeletons, just a few notches in that bedpost. But a goodie girl like you wouldn't know a damn thing about that, would ya? You're too busy doing what everyone tells you. This little bucket list of yours is the only secret that you have."

"Just stay out of my way this semester, got it?"

I didn't wait for her reply, not that I cared. I turned and went back to my room, cringing when I heard her door slam shut. Pulling out my desk chair, I sat down and hunched over, hanging my head between my knees.

God, when did I become such an asshole? She deserved zero of the shit I threw at her, but for some reason, I just couldn't help myself. I was lashing out at the closest thing to me and she just so happened to be it.

I'd almost feel bad if she didn't give it back to me just as hard. I knew I couldn't just kick her out because Link would follow through on his promise to tell Tracy. And she was the last person in the world that I wanted to disappoint. She didn't deserve anything but happiness.

My phone rang in the distance and I shot up from the seat to grab it from the nightstand. It was Tracy's custom ringtone and I promised never to miss one of her calls.

"Hey, Mom."

"Hi, sweet boy. How are you today?"

I knew I could lie and tell her everything was okay, but she made us promise after we were adopted always to tell her the truth, even if it would hurt someone we loved.

"Um. . . it's been a rough day so far."

"Oh, well, I'm sorry to hear that. Would you like to come over and help me get dinner ready for the night with my boys? I'm making stuffed shells. Maybe you call tell me all about it and you'll feel better." She had no idea that just hearing her warm motherly tone was already helping to clear my mind.

"I'll take a rain check on the discussion, but I'd like to come over and help."

"Great. I'll see you when you get here."

Mom's kitchen was my sanctuary. It was the place where I felt peace more than anywhere else did in the world. I remember the first time I came here, to this unfamiliar place that smelled like a candle store. I did everything I could to remind myself that I didn't belong here, that this was only temporary. Two people already had a handful of children living under their roof, and I had no reason to be there. But no matter how hard I tried to get them to hate me, as so many previous families had told me, they didn't. Then Tracy said to me that being in their family made their house a home, finally. It was the first time I remembered taking a real breath. I had a family, even if they didn't know who I was.

"Hey, sweetie," Mom said as I walked through the side door directly into the kitchen, grabbing a pink apron along the way and tying it around my waist. I leaned down and kissed her soft cheek as I stepped over to the sink to wash my hands. She had already started kneading the dough for the homemade shells, so I started the filling and the sauce.

"Anything you want to talk about?" she asked after a minute passed of silence. She went longer than I expected her to. The corners of my mouth lifted in a smile, knowing she wanted to gossip.

"No, ma'am."

I laughed as she harrumphed and mumbled under her breath as I went to grab the ingredients out of the fridge. Together we worked for a couple of hours until my brothers started arriving. Since Link showed up with Tyler, they were forced to set the table.

"The girls are bringing a friend. Please set a place for her," Mom called out to the boys as I pulled the dish from the oven. I assumed this was the girl they were whispering over at Friday's dinner. I never paid close enough attention to either Ford or Archer's girlfriends, but I wondered if this one was a hottie. I was definitely looking for a distraction tonight.

Placing the dish in the center of the table, I took my seat and waited for the rest of the group to join. One by one they took their seats until only three open seats remained, one of them being across from me.

"They're pulling in now," Ford said as he placed his phone back in his pocket and went to greet them at the door. Jolee and Sarah strolled in first, and I wasn't sure what I expected from the friend, maybe one that was as beautiful as the two girls but watching my new roommate shuffle in wearing a pale pink sundress was not it.

Mechanically my fist clenched around the fork in my hand. What was Keeley doing here and why was she glancing around like she wanted to be anywhere else?

"Keeley, good to see you, dear." Mom stood from her chair to greet the newcomer.

"Wait, you know her?" I asked, dumbstruck.

"Of course, I do. She came to the cookout with Sarah this summer and she was at the animal shelter fundraiser. If I recall, you missed both events."

Yes, because I was busy playing ball or practicing so that I wasn't a burden on the family.

Mom instructed Keeley to the seat across from me and I sneered in her direction as she allowed Link to pass her the pasta dish.

"This looks great, Dr. Fincher," Keeley said warmly, which grated on my nerves even more. Why did she have to fit in so perfectly with my family and her friends?

That was when it hit me; Keeley was the friend Jolee and Sarah had been discussing at dinner on Friday.

I slammed my fork onto the ceramic plate as my mom thanked Keeley for her compliment.

"You're the fucking girl that those two were talking about?" I asked as I stood from my chair and pointed toward my brother's girlfriends.

"I don't. . ."she began, but I didn't let her finish as I turned toward the women at the other end of the table. "What kinds of friends are you that you didn't even know where she has been living for what, two weeks? Jesus, selfish much? All you could do was think about yourselves." I noticed the tears building up in both of their eyes. The light from the chandelier above the table glistened in the pools. Both Ford and Archer straightened their backs, ready to defend their ladies.

"I can take care of myself," Keeley chimed in and I turned my angered gaze back in her direction.

"Right, that's why Link had to threaten you to live with me."

"She's living with you?" Sarah asked, the alarm in her voice palpable in the small dining space. "Are you okay with that?" It was evident that she was asking Keeley by the way she changed her tone from angry to empathetic.

Before Keeley could respond, I exclaimed, "What about me? I'm the one that got forced to have an unwanted female roommate all because you are both too busy with your own lives to notice that you screwed her over." I was too far gone in my anger to care about the hurt on their faces. It was apparent I had hit the mark because the guilt was there in their expressions.

"I don't need you to stand up for me. I can handle things myself."

In disbelief I stared at her, eyes unblinking. Her voice tried to sound strong and capable, but it was clear she was anything but.

"You know what? I have better things to do tonight. Enjoy your family dinner." Moving around the table, I placed a kiss on Mom's head, ignoring her calling my name, and left the house without a backward glance. I was more than thankful that I drove myself.

And when I got back to the apartment, I immediately shut myself back in my bedroom, but then thought better of it and went into Keeley's room to find her book of secrets.

I waited like a stalker on the couch for her return. A speech was planned where I would tell her that she was not allowed to infiltrate my family and that she needed to start looking for another place to live. But that moment never came.

Heat radiated on my face and I flinched as the sunlight shone through the shades on the sliding glass doors of the balcony. I sat up, my spine creaking with the movement as I stretched. Realizing that I had fallen asleep on the couch, I checked the time and then listened for any movement in the apartment. I wouldn't put it past Keeley to sneak in without disturbing me.

Double-checking, I walked down the hall, peered inside Keeley's room, and noticed it was empty. Her bed hadn't been touched.

Well, fuck, I almost felt bad that she hadn't returned last night. Almost. She had no right to infringe on my family dinner night, and she couldn't have been oblivious enough not to realize that was where she was going. I didn't share my family with anyone, especially a girl that was a temporary blip. I'd had enough of those.

This girl was so tangled up in my world that I couldn't think straight. All I knew was that my nightmares had changed since she waltzed into my life and apartment. I was in them, but they weren't directly related to me. They had been about a faceless person that I couldn't save. And that was another can of worms that I had zero desire to open.

Grabbing my cell phone out of my back pocket, I noticed that my battery was about to die as I deleted the numerous messages that I had from my brothers. Mom knew better than to reach out to me when I was in a rage. My brothers hadn't learned yet. The red battery in the corner of my phone screen mocked me as I considered hunting down Keeley's number just to make sure that she was okay. Not that I cared, of course.

Link had a private investigator friend who helped Ford track down information about his father and my finger hovered over his number. Just as I was about to connect the call, the door to the apartment opened. My eyes narrowed on the pale pink dress that was now burned into my memory.

"Where the fuck have you been?"

RENEE HARLESS

CHAPTER FIVE

KEELEY

After spending the night tossing and turning on the couch at Archer and Sarah's apartment and listening to things a friend should never have to hear, I rose with the light of dawn. I was exhausted, not just from the sleepless night, the dinner, or preparing for school to start, but my life situation in general. Hell, I couldn't even be mad at Chance's reaction at dinner. I got it. Someone that was used to keeping to himself, keeping his life in this confined box, and having me infiltrate it with streamers and such.

Folding the blanket and placing it back on the couch, I left my friends' apartment before they woke. I didn't have a car, having hitched a ride with them after the ill-fated dinner at Dr. Fincher's house. Had I known that she was the Ridge Rogue's mother? Yes. Did I have a choice to attend? No. Sarah and Jolee had dragged me there with threats more terrifying than Link calling my father. They threatened shopping trips and a makeover. I refused either.

The walk across campus was nice. There was a chill in the air that left goosebumps on my bare arms and legs, but I wasn't uncomfortable. In actuality, feeling the cold morning air on my skin reminded me that I was alive and had the world at my feet. Well, my father's world. He was adamant that I take over the business soon. They were expanding and he was stretched thin. I didn't know much of what he traded, just that he was successful at it.

Was it my dream to take over for him? No. But when had anyone ever cared about my dreams?

As I continued my trek, I noticed the newly installed wooden boxes placed along the sidewalks. These were part of the *Leave a note, Take a note* program I'd been a part of with the school paper. It was a way for students to leave a nice or uplifting message for others while receiving one of their own. On more than one occasion, we received notes with confessions and such. My job was to sift through the good ones and leave them for the paper to publish. When they were done I'd put them in the take a note section of the box. The students seemed to like the concept and so did I. It was my small way to bring happiness to a random stranger. I made a mental note to reach out to Colleen with the paper to see when she wanted me to start sifting through the letters.

The apartment complex came into sight and I hesitated. There was no saying what kind of mood Chance would be in, and I was so beyond tired that fighting was the last thing that I wanted. Maybe I'd be able to sneak through the door and head right into my bedroom. It was unlikely, that man had better hearing than anyone I knew. It made me wonder about the nickname he bestowed upon me – little mouse. I knew I wasn't as attractive as my friends. I was pale with mousy brown hair, which would explain it all. But I felt like, to Chance, the name meant something different.

But what did I know? To him, I was just an annoyance that was in his way of singledom.

I climbed the stairs in the complex and stopped in front of the apartment door. My hand hovered over the knob as I took a deep breath.

"Where the fuck have you been?" I heard as I opened the door and slipped inside. I didn't want to fight this morning and I hung my head in defeat. All I wanted was to catch a few hours of sleep, take a shower, and get all my things ready for classes that would start on Wednesday.

With a heavy sigh, I pleaded with Chance. "Can we not right now? I'm exhausted and would like to grab a couple hours of sleep."

I could feel his eyes boring into me as he stared. Looking up at him was not an option. Either I would break down into tears because he left me ragged and drained after the fight at his mom's house last night, or I'd start up another argument. I wasn't even sure what we fought about most of the time. Hell, most people and classmates thought I was pleasant enough; he just infuriated me with his cocky attitude and his "better-than-thou" opinion. Not that I could blame him. If I grew up having everyone fall at my feet, I'd probably be cocky as hell too.

Shuffling across the floor, I made my way to my bedroom, shutting the door behind me and falling face-first into the bed. I was a bit chilly, but I didn't have enough energy to care about grabbing the blanket at the end of my bed.

When I woke, I glanced around the room to remember where I was. Sometimes, I could barely remember what day or time it was when I slept too hard. Sitting up in bed, my blanket pooled around my waist and I tried to recall if I grabbed it before falling asleep. A memory of a little girl waking with a blanket wrapped around her as she shivered in the corner popped into my mind. I didn't know who she was, but she felt familiar. Something inside of me yearned to remember more, but then at the same time, I was terrified. I didn't have many memories from before I turned six. Some kids remembered their first day of kindergarten, but it was all blank to me. The doctor my father took me to had said it wasn't uncommon. He would say that nothing memorable had happened that I wanted to remember.

I never thought about it again as a kid, assuming it was the same for everyone. But now I wasn't so sure. Maybe if Chance didn't want to rip my head off later, I could ask him. After the blow-up last night, I was still on shaky terms with Sarah and Jolee. They were upset that I didn't tell them that I had been practically homeless and I was upset that they didn't take more of an initiative to find out. Yes, I was being childish, but so were they. Sometimes I was jealous of the perfect little lives they had been creating. They both had their own issues, but I was headed for a future entirely carved out for me with no say in any of it.

Swiping my hand across my face I stood up on shaky legs, removed my sandals, and hobbled over to the bathroom. I hadn't been drinking, but I felt like I was on my way to being three sheets to the wind. That usually happened when my anxiety was at a high level. Living with my ticking time bomb of a roommate would do that.

Blindly I unzipped the back of my dress. It floated down my body into a pool of petal pink at my feet. Stepping out of the bunched material, I tossed my bra and panties on top of the pile. Reaching across the shower curtain, I turned on the faucet as hot as it would go, sighing with relief when the steam began to fill the small space.

Stepping under the hot spray, I let my head fall forward, my hair draping around my head like a curtain as the beads of water fell down my back. I was so utterly exhausted. Exhausted from needing to be perfect for my father, exhausted from the fear of being kicked out of school if I hadn't found a place to live, exhausted from fighting with Chance and it had only been a handful of days together. How we would survive the semester, I wasn't sure. I'd need to keep looking for another place just in case he became intolerable. The money for the rent was stashed in my wallet and I hoped to give it to him just to appease his attitude for a while.

And finally, I was exhausted from life in general. That was probably why I started making that bucket list. It wasn't that I was sick or dying in the real sense, but it sure felt that way as I looked toward my future after graduation. My father didn't even care to ask what I wanted to do with my life. I was told to get a business degree and that was that. Sometimes I wonder if he even loved me or mom. I was just the person to continue his legacy.

The steam was growing so incredibly thick in the bathroom that I could barely see in the small shower stall. My skin had grown reddish-pink from the heat. Quickly I poured shampoo into my palm and washed my hair, following up with conditioner before I lathered my loofa with body wash. The suds dripped down my body as I cleansed the skin, paying close attention to the part between my legs. I can't remember how long it had been since I'd had sex or even pleasured myself. Obviously, none of it had been memorable. It was a shame that all the back and forth with Chance always left me hot and bothered. Since Saturday morning, I'd wanted to run back to my storage unit to find my B.O.B. and take care of my frustration.

I allowed my fingers to linger along the sensitive skin of my pussy as the water washed away the soap, but I knew it wouldn't give me the release that I needed. If anything, it was only going to work me up more.

Maybe that was something I needed to add to my list. I'd always been curious about having an orgasm in public since I watched *When Harry Met Sally*. I made a mental note to add public sexuality to my list.

Knowing that my time in the shower was running out, I turned off the faucet. Wet hair dripped down my back as I blindly reached out for my towel, but my hand came up empty.

"Dammit," I huffed as I slipped my head past the shower curtain and surveyed the bathroom. There was not a single towel in sight except the lone hand towel. That little thing wouldn't even dry the skin under my breasts.

Wringing out my hair as much as I could, I stepped out of the shower and skipped across the floor mats so that I didn't leave too many puddles on the floor. It seemed like something that would piss Chance off.

Giving myself a pep talk, I looked in the fogged-up mirror and said, "You can do this. It's right across the hall and he won't even hear you." Swiping my hand across the glass, I blinked at myself in the mirror, taking in the day-old eye makeup that had smeared under my eyes. With a quick swipe from my index fingers, that issue was quickly remedied.

Turning around, I twisted the knob and opened the door with my head down, hoping to hide and quickly make my way across the hall. I should have known that nothing would have gone as planned.

The moment my feet stepped beyond the bathroom threshold; my face collided with a hot wet wall. A hot wet wall that was moving.

"Oh my god!" I screamed as I stood straighter, the top of my head colliding with a solid chin. The pain reverberated throughout my body, but I couldn't take the time to fathom any of it because I was too busy trying to cover my oversized breasts and the unwaxed part between my legs.

"Geez, calm down," the half-naked wall said to me. I blinked and stared at the ridges of his abdomen, the same ones that were flashing like neon lights, blinking to draw my eye to the tent forming in his basketball shorts.

"I'm naked!" I yelled in a whisper as if everyone else in the complex could hear me. I finally pulled my gaze away from his growing erection to look up at his smug face. He even had the audacity to place his hands on my upper arms. I wasn't sure if it was to keep me in place or to push me away.

"That you are." There was a huskiness to his voice that dripped down my body with each word, leaving me a wobbly mess in his hold. I was utterly hypnotized as he licked his lips, Chance's eyes took inventory of each inch of my body.

"I. . .uh. . .forgot a towel."

"You look a little dazed. I bet your nipples are hard right now."

"I'm cold," I tried to argue, but it came out sounding more like a question.

"Naw," he said, his fingers gently trailing up and down my arms in various shapes, leaving heated paths in their wake. "I think you're turned on standing here with me. I think there is a little wild side to you, mouse."

Licking my lips, I asked him, "Why do you call me that? Mouse?"

Of course, instead of answering, he shrugged his shoulders. He created a path from my collarbone to the middle of my breasts with his fingertip.

"I have something I want to discuss with you. So why don't you go ahead and get dressed."

Somehow he had me so mesmerized that I completely forgot that I was showing him all of me in the sunlight.

"Oh my god!"

Chance leaned forward, the sweaty ends of his hair dropping onto my shoulder as his lips caressed my ear. I tried to pull away, but he held me in place as he took his fill of me. I was pretty sure that I could reach an orgasm from just his possessive stare alone.

"Now we're even."

He released his hold on me and strutted back to his room with the muscles in his back working with each step. Why did he have to be so damn good-looking? Not even his attitude diminished his attractiveness. I stood there like a carved statue until Chance shouted from his room that I was still naked.

"Shit!" I exclaimed as I spun around and almost rammed my face into the trim surrounding my door opening. Once I safely made it over the threshold, I slammed the door and searched around the dressers for something comfortable to slip into. Not sexy, but actually comfortable, like a T-shirt and boxer shorts.

My phone buzzed with a message from Colleen from the paper. Our project with the note boxes across campus was launching tomorrow for the second year and she wanted me to stop by in the morning to grab some pre-existing notes to leave in the "take a note" section. We were promoting the boxes as a place to put a secret confession or ask for advice. While Colleen and I messaged back and forth, I grabbed an envelope, stashed the cash I had withdrawn for rent, and shoved it inside. If Chance and I were going to call a truce of sorts (yeah, right), then I would make sure that he was going to treat me like an actual roommate.

Sealing the flap, I held the envelope in my hand, tapping it against my bare thigh as I contemplated how to walk out of the room. I should probably feel embarrassed that Chance saw me naked, felt my wet skin against his, scrutinized every inch of me. But for some reason, I felt empowered.

The wet ends of my hair had started to seep through my shirt as I stood there deciding my next move. Now I knew that my nipples were hard from the cold water. And of course, I hadn't put on a bra.

"Time is wasting!" his voice called out from somewhere in the apartment and it knocked me into gear.

Opening the door, I stepped into the hallway. There was noise coming from the kitchen as I made my way to the living room, prepared for battle, but knowing I was already losing the fight. Because Chance Fincher had called a truce, I wasn't sure what that would entail.

CHAPTER SIX

CHANCE

Coming home from a two-hour gym workout and running into a naked Keeley was not what I had expected, but it was a pleasant surprise after collecting the mail and finding three letters addressed to Elliot Winslow. I immediately threw them in the trash without a second thought.

I didn't even want to think about the skinny guy that called himself her boyfriend and was adamant about seeing Keeley. When he started saying his name was Thomas, or Timmy, or something with a T, I cut him off. Just him being at my door annoyed me. Now he was the sole reason I wanted to hit the gym anyway. What had she ever seen in a cocky bastard like him?

Reminiscing about my roommate's state of undress took my mind off the visitor. I had been curious to see those curves she kept tucked away behind baggy clothes, especially after seeing her wear the form-fitting dress last night at dinner.

Now I wasn't even sure why I disliked her so much. I fought with her because she was there. Now I wondered if it was because I was attracted to her. I couldn't even deny it since my cock was still standing at attention beneath my gym shorts.

After leaving her standing, I contemplated rubbing out a quick one when I stepped into my room, but I knew that I didn't have time for that. I had a proposition for her that came to me while at the gym. I also had a lot of questions regarding her father and his business.

I assumed that she would take a few minutes to dress and do whatever women did after a shower and thought I'd be able to take a quick one myself. Chucking my shorts and briefs in the corner, I dashed to the bathroom in my birthday suit, because I had nothing to be ashamed of, and stepped into a cold shower with the hopes to get my erection down.

It didn't diminish it entirely, but I was at least able to keep him in check as I tucked him in a pair of boxer briefs and then covered up with a set of blue basketball shorts. Glancing at my phone from where it was charging on my nightstand, I noticed that I had my usual amount of missed messages from my family and from random women. I also noticed that it was still a bit early for lunch, but I didn't care.

I could still smell Keeley's flowery shampoo that lingered in the air even after my shower as I walked past her room. How had it only been a couple of days since she was thrust into my life? My little mouse had been homeless and Link saved the day, as he usually did.

She was such a timid little thing until I got her fired up. I had started making it my new goal.

In the kitchen, I got out the mixings for a salad and some salmon I had picked up. With my grueling practice schedule, I needed to keep lean meals available at any time.

As I tossed the salmon into the water to poach it, I hollered out to Keeley that she was wasting time. It took only another couple of minutes before she came back out looking as nervous as always. She regarded me with a fearful look, like she was waiting for the attack.

"I'm making some lunch," I told her, hoping to ease her troubled look.

"You cook?"

I glanced up at her as she walked toward the kitchen counter peninsula and took a seat on one of the barstools, placing a white non-descript envelope on the counter. She looked so young and innocent with an oversized white T-shirt that seemed to be soaking wet from her hair. I could make out the dusky pink color of her nipples through the damp material. To distract myself from reaching out, ripping off the shirt, and discovering what her nipples tasted like, I turned back to the stove and checked on the fish.

"Yes, I like to cook. I'm making a poached salmon mixed salad for us."

"Oh," she said, surprised. I'm sure she didn't expect me to feed her after the fights we've had. "Did you add a dash of poison?"

"Ah, not this time," I joked. "But I'd be on the lookout. This will be just a few more minutes, but I wanted to run something by you."

She settled more onto the stool and fingered the envelope toward me. "Before you begin, I wanted to make sure I paid my fair share. So, this is what I can pay toward rent right now. If you need more or need me to give toward utilities, please tell me."

A sneer grew on my face as if the envelope would jump out and bite me.

"I don't want your money."

"Too bad. I'm giving it to you. I'm not a freeloader."

"No, Keeley."

"Yes, Chance."

There was a determination in her eyes that I couldn't overlook and I admired it. Reaching out for the envelope, I pulled it toward me.

"Fine. I'll take it. Now, I wanted to start by saying that I don't have anything against you personally. I just don't like being forced into something. Especially when it messes with my. . .extracurriculars."

"Your brother didn't leave me much of a choice. My father didn't need to be made aware of my living predicament."

"Right. Your father is a topic we're going to revisit." Turning around, I grabbed the bowls of salad and placed the poached salmon on top, then slid one of the bowls over to her, followed by a fork. "Okay, so you know that little bucket list that you have?"

"Yes," she replied begrudgingly. "I really wish that you hadn't been snooping."

"Well, I don't know about that, it may work out for you in the end. I'm going to help you check off as many items on the list as we can."

I looked up at her from my lunch and watched as she seemed to choke on the salad. Covering her mouth with a shaking hand she said, "I'm sorry, what?"

"Your bucket list. I want to help you with it."

"Why?" she asked curiously. "What's in it for you?"

"I don't know. The possibility of watching you step out of your comfort zone. And let's not forget the chance at seeing you get embarrassed."

"I'm guessing that there is a catch." Her eyes narrowed as she gazed at me. If she only knew the things I wanted in return, those pale cheeks of hers would turn bright red.

"Of course, there is. I want to know why you're doing what your father wants. At least that's what I gathered from your phone call."

"You listened to my conversation?"

Rolling my eyes, I took another bite of my salad. "You weren't exactly quiet."

"Okay, I'll answer your questions. Anything else?"

"I'm glad you asked. I need a tutor this year to help keep me on track with my classes while I have baseball practice and games. And I've decided that tutor will be you."

"What if I don't want to be your. . .academic advisor?"

"That's not really an option because we'd just go back to fighting and all that fighting makes me work up an appetite."

"I'm not having sex with you, Chance."

I couldn't help but chuckle. She thought that I had regular vanilla sex with women.

"I don't have sex; I fuck, hard. And when I have you, because let's both be honest with ourselves, it will happen; you will beg me for it. I want to own every part of you, little mouse."

Keeley pushed aside her salad and dropped her head into her hands. "I'm so confused right now."

Don't worry, sweetheart. So am I.

"What's there to be confused about? We call a truce, I help you with your bucket list, you answer my questions about your family, and you help me with school."

"Don't forget to add that you expect to have sex with me."

"I told you, I don't expect it; I just know it's going to happen. You can't tell me that you don't feel the tension here."

"I feel something. Pretty sure it's indigestion and not tension," Keeley added as she jumped down from the stool and grabbed her salad bowl.

"Don't fool yourself, Keeley."

"Why do I feel like I'm getting more out of this than you. What's the catch? What aren't you telling me?" I could see where she was coming from. Looking from the outside in, she was getting to do things that would be life-changing, whereas I was getting some information and help in school.

"No catch. But if you want to go back to fighting, I'm good with that. I can already tell you that your ex-boyfriend, I think that's who he said he was, is a douchebag. He gave me enough material to roast you with for the next month."

"Thomas came by?"

"Is that his name?" I thought about the preppy, polo-wearing jerk that stopped by while she was sleeping. He had said that she was expecting him, but I knew that he was lying right away. Pansy couldn't even make eye contact with me. I didn't like him at all and had no idea how he landed Keeley. "I sent him on his way. That's all you need to worry about."

"Thank you," she said as she left the kitchen area with her bowl still in her hands. I followed and found her settling on the couch. I typically didn't allow food to be eaten on the sofa, but I figured that I'd let it slide this one time. "I'm not sure how he figured out I was staying here, so I appreciate the deterrent."

"Is he going to be a problem?"

"I don't know. I hope not, but he seems pretty persistent in getting back together."

I could tell by her voice and expression that getting back together with him was the last thing that she wanted. She spoke of him the same way she spoke of her father. And I had never even heard her mention her mother.

"I'll make sure he leaves you alone, if you want."

"Really?" she asked in surprise, her brows rising in a high arch that caused lines across her forehead.

"Yeah, I'm not always an asshole. Mom taught me to be a gentleman, sometimes."

"Maybe while I'm divulging about my father you can tell me about your family dynamic. I only know bits and pieces from Jolee and Sarah."

Instantly I saw red as the anger exploded. I hated when people asked about our family. It wasn't usually because they were curious, but because they were looking for a way to gossip or sink their claws into one of us. But I could sense Keeley was asking innocently.

It took me a couple of seconds to pull myself out of the fog, and Keeley had already gone back to eating her salad.

"So, I think there are a couple of things we can tackle right away on your list: the double date, growing a pair of balls and asking someone on a date, learning to cook a meal. There are a few we can do at once, but I'll leave those as a surprise."

Leaning forward, Keeley placed her bowl on the coffee table then turned to face me. She looked so serious, like the weight of the world was on her shoulders and she had nothing to help bear the load.

"Okay. I'll let you help me with my list and I agree to tutor you."

"What about my questions?"

She narrowed her eyes as she nodded. "I don't know why you care so much that my life has been laid out for me with a specific plan to follow. Most of the students here are in the same predicament."

"Maybe I want to know what motivated you to create the list at all."

"Okay, when do you want to start?" she inquired as she grabbed our empty salad bowls and stood.

"Today. We have lunch plans with your friends."

I left Keeley with specific instructions for today, but I wouldn't know if she followed through until later. Unlike the pink dress she wore at my mother's house for dinner, Keeley donned a denim skirt that hit her mid-thigh and a blue button-down sleeveless shirt that she tied at the waist. Her hair was tied back in her typical ponytail and I yanked the tie loose from the strands as she passed by me leaving the apartment. I was ready for her to retaliate as I drove us to lunch, but she held back.

I could tell Keeley was getting worried as we drove into a part of Boston that most students didn't venture. One of our favorite places to dine was a hidden secret. It was older, surrounded by large brownstones, but not a sign of a restaurant. Mom knew the owners, so we tried to come out as often as possible, especially my brothers and me.

With the radio playing a rock song at a low volume, I waited for her to ask where we were, but she remained silent. I couldn't help but wonder why she was trusting me. Because let's be honest, I was an asshole ninety-nine percent of the time, but I knew how to treat a woman right.

"We're here," I told her as I found a place to park and turned off the car. "The others already grabbed a table."

"I don't know where here is, but I'm starving, so let's go."

Thankfully she waited for me to make my way around the car and open her door. If this was going to be a double date of sorts, which she had on her list, then I was going to go all out. Tucking her hand into the crook of my arm, I escorted her across the street and down an alleyway. We arrived at a backdoor where a large guard stood watch. He recognized me immediately and ushered us inside, where I felt Keeley instantly relax. There was something about the restaurant that made you feel right at home. It was quite the hidden gem.

"This place is. . ."she whispered, taking it all in as I escorted her toward our table.

Smiling down at her, I replied, "I know. It's really special. Our table is over here."

She noticed the two of the four people sitting at the table and squealed in delight, bouncing on my arm with each step. As I expected, Jolee and Sarah launched themselves at Keeley when we reached them. I went ahead and took a seat at the long table, leaving an open spot for Keeley. I may have felt guilty about the strain between her friendship with my brothers' girlfriends after dinner on Sunday and my outburst. I attempted to make amends.

Ignoring my brothers and their smirking gazes, I focused on the three females as they hugged, Jolee and Sarah apologizing more than once. I wasn't going to pretend that I understood women or their dynamics, but apparently, they had forgiven each other. As the girls took their seats, Keeley surprised everyone by sitting in the empty chair beside me, reaching over and wrapping her arms around my shoulders in an embrace.

"Thank you," she whispered in my ear, and fuck if my cock didn't twitch at her breath brushing across the sensitive skin.

We ordered drinks, both Keeley and I opting for water while the others ordered beer and cocktails. The conversation flowed. Most of it focused on the upcoming school year and our plans after graduation. Ford had already graduated and started a Master's program, Jolee and I were set to snag our diplomas this year, and Keeley, Archer, and Sarah had more credits to put under their belts. Although Keeley was ahead on her classes and said that she may be able to graduate early. I wondered if that was her father's doing.

Everyone at the table relaxed as the food arrived; a lunch-sized portion of duck confit for me and scallops for Keeley. It didn't take long before the girls retreated to the bathroom in a group. My brothers chose that moment to launch their interrogation.

"You and Keeley," Ford started. His initiating the conversation irked me more than it should. I'd glanced at Keeley through lunch and her eyes drifted toward my brother. It made me wonder if she had a crush on him. That would be against both brother and friend code if she acted on it.

"No. I'm just helping her with something."

"With what? She's the girls' friend, Chance," Archer stated as he joined in.

"I know who she is. We called a truce and she asked me to help her with a few things. Plus, she's going to tutor me this year. See? No problems."

I could sense the skepticism from my brothers and it hurt more than they could imagine. But I'd never let on. Despite my playboy ways, I was always respectful toward women, unlike Archer, famous for gaslighting, and Ford, who had a more sordid reputation.

Luckily, the women chose that moment to return to the table. Their smiles were broad and there was a cheerful pep in their steps. Across the table, my brothers kissed their women on their cheeks while I turned toward Keeley and whispered, "Did you follow my instructions one-hundred percent?"

Keeley leaned forward to take a sip of her water, then turned her head so that our eyes connected and she gave a slight nod.

While everyone else ordered another set of drinks and the music volume in the room turned up as the dinner crowd gave way to the bar group, I dropped my hand from the table and placed it on Keeley's warm thigh.

I had assumed that she would move her leg or push my hand away, but Keeley kept surprising me. She twisted her hips so that her knees were slanted toward me, which caused my hand to slide farther up her thigh.

My little mouse wanted to play.

CHAPTER SEVEN

KEELEY

Here I was sitting at a restaurant with my friends, without panties, and allowing this Ridge Rogue to glide his hand up my leg. The feel of his rough fingers on my thigh did something to me. It flipped a switch that had all rational thoughts leaving my body.

I wasn't sure if the people across from me could tell what Chance was doing, but the moment his fingertips touched my soft wet folds, I didn't even care. My legs jerked in reaction, wanting to close and keep his hand there for eternity.

The conversation had been flowing around me, but I was too lost in wanting more from Chance until he turned to look at me. Then I was suddenly nervous as everyone's eyes were pinned on me and I tried to recall what they had been discussing.

Thankfully Chance chose that moment to chime in. "My schedule is *spread* pretty thin this semester. What about you, Keeley?" With the way he emphasized the word spread, I instinctively knew that he wanted me to stretch my legs open. There was no chance at me disobeying him. I opened up until my knee touched his. We were sitting so close that he looked as if his arm was resting on his own leg.

Licking my lips, I replied, playing his word game, "I have a pretty *tight* schedule of classes. There weren't many options."

"Seems to me like you work too much," he said as he slid his hand up and down my slit before slipping a digit into my sex. I had to bite the inside of my cheek to keep from moaning in pleasure. I could already tell he would live up to his reputation. "Maybe you need to find a way to *let go* more often."

Soon his thumb joined in and ran circles around my clit. The tight bundle of nerves sent electric waves through my body.

"Yes!" Sarah exclaimed. "Keeley is so wound up. You need to let loose more often." Chance's answering chuckle would usually have irritated me, but

I was lost in the feeling of his hand bringing me pleasure that I chose to ignore it.

"Have you ever seen Keeley let loose?" Chance asked Sarah as my inner walls began to quiver. I clenched my hands onto the sides of my chair to try and maintain my dignity.

"You know, now that you mention it, I've never seen her so much as get drunk."

"Well, maybe we can change that. What do you think, Keeley? Want to go *over the edge*?" Him and those deft fingers were going to be too much as I nodded and turned my face toward his. Chance continued to rub my clit and I swear I saw sparkling lights flicker before my eyes. Except I didn't want to have my first orgasm in forever sitting at a table in front of my friends. Jerking back my chair, I stood up, forcing a smile as Chance's hand fell from my lap.

"Excuse me," I mumbled as I made my way toward the bathroom. I couldn't hear what was said; I just knew I needed to find a secluded place to finish myself off. Female blue balls were real, and I did not want to succumb to them.

I shoved the women's bathroom door open and immediately made my way to the sink. *Was I really going to do this? Was I going to get myself off in the bathroom of an exclusive restaurant all because Chance*

Fincher was a master with his fingers? I took in my red cheeks and glistening eyes and immediately knew my answer. *Yes, yes I was.*

Turning around, I planned to select one of the two empty stalls when the bathroom door began to open. Mumbled curses flew from my mouth at the disappointment of knowing that the newcomer had thwarted my chance at a release. But instead of a female, I was surprised to see Chance waltz into the bathroom.

"What are you doing in here?" I asked as he approached, my backward steps trapping me against the long concrete counter that held the two sinks.

"I decided to come help you."

"Oh. Won't they suspect something?" I questioned as his strong arms lifted me onto the counter. My hands flew out to brace myself against his shoulders.

"I told them your ex was harassing you and you received a text from him." Chance spoke the words, but his attention was solely on his two hands sliding up my bare legs, pushing the skirt up to my waist as he went. "Fuck, you have a pretty pussy." As if possessed, he slid his hands from the outside of my thighs towards the apex, his thumbs caressing my wet plump center.

My body jerked at the first contact and a wicked smile grew on his lips.

"Chance. Someone could come in." My concern was only half-hearted. I wanted my release more than I wanted my next breath.

"Good. That's what I'm hoping for."

The tall, dark-haired devil knelt on the dingy bathroom floor and, before I could utter another word, pulled my hips forward and dove between my legs like his life depended on it.

"Oh my god!" I cried out when his tongue slid between my folds, his teeth scratching against my swollen button.

"Jesus Christ, you taste good," he said as he pulled back a smidge, then he dove right back in. My body jerked as his grip tightened around my thighs, the back of my head colliding with the mirror. I saw stars, but it wasn't from the head injury, it was from Chance's complete and utter domination of my pussy.

Somewhere in the distance, I heard a hinge squeak, quickly followed by an "Oh my," but I never noticed if she left. My orgasm came rushing forward, and before I could take my next breath, my hand reached out blindly and gripped Chance's hair, holding him in place as I exploded against his mouth.

As I came down from my high, I slowly released my clutch on Chance's hair, only just registering the press of his lips against my thigh as he stood up.

"Can I sign up for the next one?" the distant voice from earlier said with much more clarity. My cheeks burned as I realized that she had been witness to my explosive orgasm, but before I could turn my attention in her direction, Chance stood to his full height and locked his gaze with mine.

"Leave," he commanded, directed at our visitor. My release still coated his lips and chin leaving a sheen on his skin from the lights. I liked him like this. Even though I had been on the receiving end of pleasure, he looked exactly like I felt.

After the sound of the door closing, Chance leaned closer and said, "You look good like this, spread out for me to feast on you. My new favorite meal. May need to have it three times a day."

Silence fell between us as the level of our newly acquired friendship shifted. Then the buzzing of a phone shattered the rose-colored glasses we were both wearing. Chance reached into his back pocket without taking his eyes off mine. His stare was so unnerving that I glanced down at the phone as he tried to power down the screen. The name Magnolia flashed brightly before it went dark.

Her name was the splash of cold water that I needed. What was I doing letting Chance, my new roommate, take care of me in a restroom?

"I can see the wheels spinning. Don't overthink it, Keeley. I just knocked three things off your list: a double date, public nudity, and an orgasm not given by yourself. When we get back to the apartment, I have three questions to ask you."

"But. . .you said. . ." I was so confused. He had said something so possessive and delicious right after our visitor left, then he did a complete one-eighty when his phone rang.

"I think we should head back out or our friends will wonder what we're doing. I'll go out first."

Chance turned around and exited the bathroom without a backward glance as I continued to sit on the cold concrete countertop with my skirt bunched around my waist.

The car ride back to the apartment was as silent as it had been once I returned to the table after Chance's and my rendezvous in the bathroom. I still wasn't sure how he convinced his brothers and my friends that I was busy arguing with my ex on the phone, but they had bought it hook, line, and sinker. I was afraid that the girls would see the thrill of my release all over my face, but that hadn't been the case. They had the haziness of a buzz running through their veins.

When the car pulled up to the apartment complex, Chance killed the engine and jumped out of the vehicle like his heels were on fire. I was left sitting in the passenger seat, both tired and confused, afraid I had done something wrong. Had we suddenly fallen back into the enemies category or were we still in an unsteady friendship?

On shaky legs, I stepped out of the car and shut the door, making sure it was locked on the inside. He may be an asshole ninety percent of the time, but I didn't want his car broken into.

He wasn't waiting in the complex's lobby when I arrived, so I decided to kill time and stop by the mailbox even though I was pretty sure it would be empty. Surprisingly I found several envelopes; many addressed to an Elliott Winslow and some to Chance Fincher. I assumed Elliott was a previous tenant. Sarah and I used to get old tenants' mail daily. How I missed living with Sarah when things weren't always so problematic.

Gathering the envelopes, I trudged my way up the three flights of stairs until I stood in front of the apartment door in my denim skirt and a sleeveless shirt that seemed so silly looking back. I'm not sure what I expected from Chance, but a complete blow-off wasn't it; though it should have been. I had taken his threat of not wearing panties and taken it a step further by not wearing a bra. A lot of good that did me. The shirt had been rubbing my overly sensitive nipples into hard peaks.

Reaching between the unbuttoned halves of my shirt, I fingered the delicate chain necklace that rested between the breast. I only took it off when I showered or wore a revealing outfit. It was the only piece of me from before I could remember. Dad liked to tell me it was a camp gift, but I knew that it was more than that deep in my heart. There was something significant in the intertwined hearts despite being fake and turned my skin green if I showered wearing it. But it was my talisman, my center, my Zen.

When I finally got a hold of myself, I reached out for the doorknob at the same time the door flung open. My body shifted forward and I fell into Chance's chest again, just as I had two days before. Only this time, I wasn't naked.

There may be some sort of higher being, after all.

"You don't have to throw yourself at me, Keeley." He joked as he helped to set me upright. "A normal guy would apologize for storming off, but we both know that's not me. Then I figured you were probably pissed at me anyway and I decided to keep my distance. Don't want you swinging a bat at me again."

I wasn't sure what to say as I let him readjust my position, not clinging to his body any longer. My inner vixen missed his touch.

"You okay, little mouse?" he asked as he looked down at me with concern in his eyes. It was the first time I had seen that kind of genuine emotion from him. I had already begun to notice that he used anger as a front. It was his defense mechanism to keeping people at a distance he was comfortable with. I wondered if he even knew that he did it.

"Yeah. . .um. . ." I started and licked my lips before I continued. "I was checking the mail. It looks like you're getting mail from a previous tenant, an Elliott Winslow."

Chance's face paled at the name, and I watched as his Adam's apple bobbed from a forced swallow. "Yeah, I have a pile of them in the kitchen." He turned around to walk back into the apartment and I dutifully followed.

I knew my time in the interrogation chair was coming, but I wasn't ready.

"Do you think you can shelf the family questions for another day?" I wanted to plead with him, but I knew I didn't have many bargaining chips after the orgasm he gave me earlier. Chance seemed very tit-for-tat.

"Not going to happen. Go ahead and make yourself comfortable. Want a beer?"

"I don't drink."

Instead of questioning me like everyone else he brought me a bottle of water and sat next to me with his bottle of craft brew.

"Hm. . .where to start?"

"Why are you so curious anyway?"

Shrugging his shoulders, Chance took a long swallow of his drink before slumping back against the sofa.

"Fine, three questions and that's it." I was putting my foot down so that he didn't think he had full access to my life.

"For now, until I check some more items off your list."

"Chance," I warned.

"Keeley," he mimicked. "What kind of business does your father run that you will be taking over?" Wow, right into the nitty-gritty.

"He's in trading."

"What kind of trading, Keeley?"

Turning to face him, I questioned if that was what he wanted to use for his second inquiry. When he nodded, I continued. "I don't know. It's an international business that he started from scratch. It's called Fox Trading."

"You're telling me that you're going to take over a business that you know nothing about?"

"I don't need to know anything about it. That's why the management-level positions are there. I'm there to make sure it all runs efficiently."

"Are those the lies you've been fed? If I were you, I'd make sure you know what you're getting into before you sign your life over."

Reaching around my neck, I fingered the delicate chain of my necklace before sliding my fingers down to the charm. I could see Chance eyeing the jewelry with interest.

"Last question."

"Why did you look so unhappy in your highschool graduation picture with your parents?"

All the air in my lungs vanished with a resounding whoosh. How could someone I barely knew notice that I had been so unhappy that day, that my world had been flipped upside and pushed off course the minutes before I had walked across the stage?

"My graduation was on my eighteenth birthday. It was the day my parents told me that I wasn't their biological daughter. I don't know the details, but there were no other relatives, so my aunt and uncle took me in.

"They had no intention of ever telling me, but all of my college applications had come back incomplete because the birth certificate I had been using was fake. That's the real reason I had to start at a community college."

Chance looked at me in a way I hadn't expected. Instead of pity or sympathy, his was one of compassion. Because if anyone knew what I had felt that day, it was probably Chance. It made me want to ask him about how he came to be adopted by Dr. Fincher, but I knew now was not that time. Hopefully, I'd get that opportunity.

"What's that you're messing with?" he inquired and it took me a minute to realize that I was fidgeting with the charm on my necklace.

"You used up your three questions," I teased, the corner of my mouth lifting. Chance's lips did the same as he shook his head slightly, pieces of his gorgeous brown hair falling over his forehead.

"Humor me."

"Fine," I said, scooting closer to him. Our knees brushed and a shiver passed down my spine at the contact. "I've had it as long as I can remember."

Chance reached for the charm and I dropped it into his palm. Our faces were mere inches apart as I watched him examine the gold trinket. He was staring at it as if he was solving a riddle, turning it back and forth in his hand. He tugged the hearts closer to his face and it jerked me toward him.

"Sorry," he apologized but made no move to release the charm.

"Is everything okay?" I asked. Something about how he was taking mental note of the necklace had me on edge. I couldn't figure out what made it so fascinating to him.

"Yeah," he said, dropping the piece so that it flung back against my chest. "You don't know where you got it?"

"Nope. Mom, er, my aunt said I had it when I came to live with her. I don't remember anything before then. I was like five."

Chance made a sound under his breath then reached for the remote.

"Want to watch a movie?"

The change of subject was jarring but not unwelcome. Tucking my legs up on the couch, I settled against the cushions and watched as Chance flipped through the movie channels. He settled on an action flick, but I wasn't going to argue with the choice. My mind couldn't focus on anything but how close we were sitting on the couch.

Three days ago, if you had asked me if I would be allowed anywhere in the apartment when Chance was present, I would have laughed in your face. But since my naked run-in, things had shifted between us.

Hell, even if what happened at the restaurant never happened again, I knew I could die a well-pleasured woman.

"Hey, Chance," I beckoned him.

"Yeah," he replied, turning toward me after a particularly intense scene in the movie.

"I think I know what the next item on my bucket list should be."

CHAPTER EIGHT

CHANCE

Keeley was sitting next to me on the couch as I put on a shoot-em-up movie I had seen far more times than I could count. I chose it on purpose because there was absolutely no way I could focus on some sort of plotline with the feel of her body heat against my skin.

Something about Keeley intrigued me, and that was after I knew I would be addicted to her distinct flavor. Pleasing a woman with my mouth and tongue was one of my favorite forms of foreplay, with a couple of hours of rough sex the endgame. But the first drop of Keeley's juices on my tongue captivated me and the typical endgame vanished. All I wanted was to send her over the edge. And it was spectacular to watch.

Something had changed my mood at lunch. I could only assume that it was my reaction to the foreplay and my lack of desire to fuck Keeley out of respect to her. It was like I had become someone different with her, and that wasn't something I could handle.

The life of Chance Fincher had to be a certain way. There were checkboxes that needed to be marked. Whenever something deviated away from those, I felt lost. I'd been Chance Fincher for seven years now and I was determined that nothing change that.

Keeley spoke up saying that she wanted to check off another item on her list. Her list had such an array of items that it was hard to know what she would pick next, but I definitely would if I could help her.

I didn't even hesitate as I turned to face her, placing my hand on her knee as I said, "What do you have in mind?"

She was speaking quite animatedly, her hands flailing around in her excitement, but I was too focused on the feel of her skin under my palm. Fuck if I didn't want to force her legs open and devour her delectable pussy again.

"Chance?" she called and I looked up from my stare on her knee.

"Sorry, I was zoning. You said something about a baseball game?"

"Yes. So, as I was saying, I thought that I could knock two things off of my list. I could ask someone to go see a Red Sox game. I was able to mark asking someone on a date and going to see a Red Sox game."

"Hm. . .that seems pretty good. Do you have tickets to a game? They're usually sold out by now since we're so close to the World Series."

"Oh," she said, disappointment evident on her face. "I hadn't thought of that."

"Don't worry, I can help. I have a few people that owe me favors."

"You don't have to. . ."

"Stop. I don't do anything I don't want to do."

"Maybe you can help me find someone to ask?

Before I could stop it, my fingers clenched on her knee. She was going to ask someone, probably a stranger, to go on a date? What the hell was wrong with me? But then, I didn't date. That wasn't my MO. I took women to bed and that was that.

Suddenly I felt like I wanted to be anywhere else but here on the couch with her enjoying the movie. There was a rage building up in me that I didn't want her to witness.

Launching myself off the couch, I barely registered the hurt in her gaze as she watched me grab my keys from the kitchen counter.

"I'll be back later."

"Chance. Chance!" she called out as I walked out of the apartment without an explanation.

Normally I'd head toward a bar on the outskirts of town and find someone to occupy my night, but despite my jealousy, I didn't want to lose the flavor of Keeley on my tongue. Instead, I made my way toward a twenty-four-hour coffee shop across the street from campus and planned on doing a little research.

I didn't even drink coffee, the flavor was far too bitter for me, but I knew from a past visit that the shop had a tea latte that I could settle for.

Drink in hand, I took a seat in a leather lounge chair situated in front of a fireplace and pulled up the search bar in my phone. Something about Keeley's father bothered me. Granted, I knew many people who had no idea what their parents did for a living, but taking over a business that you knew nothing about seemed strange. Did he trade goods, food, animals, people? That would be something an average person would figure out ahead of time.

And that necklace she wore. It seemed like a simple piece of jewelry, but the fragile gold was blinding at closer inspection. There was some sort of recognition that chimed in the back of my mind, but I couldn't put my finger on it.

But before I could delve farther into my past, someone lounged in the chair across from mine and kicked my foot in the process. I sneered up at the newcomer only to find my brother smiling wildly in my direction.

"How'd you know that I was here?" I asked him. Ford had always been the most reserved out of the brothers, so to see him so happy and carefree was a bit jarring.

"I didn't. Jolee and I were leaving the animal shelter and she wanted something to drink."

"And where is your better, and more attractive, other half?" Joking with Ford was always funny because he always answered with a scowl. When I came to live with Tracy, Ford had always been the most distant. I never let him know how much it bothered me, but since Jolee melted his frosty exterior, it seemed like he now understood how difficult he had made it for all of us brothers.

"Bathroom, then placing her order, I'm sure."

"Maybe you can help me if you have a few minutes," I said, leaning forward with my phone in hand.

Ford seemed taken aback by my request. I rarely asked my brothers for help. Growing up the way I had, I needed to be as self-sufficient as possible. For a second, I realized that maybe my detachment was why Ford had kept his distance for so long.

"Of course, what do you need?" If it were any other request, I would be alarmed at how open Ford was at helping me, but it was Keeley, and I had serious worry about what she was being led into. Something about her father's non-grin in her graduation picture irked me more than it should. He seemed. . .uncaring, calculating, like she was just another piece to his puzzle.

"I need some information. . . on Fox Trading."

"Is that Keeley's-" Ford started, but I cut him off. "Yes, it's her father's business that she's taking over. I want to know everything about it."

"Why?" he asked just as Jolee skipped over to us and launched herself onto Ford's lap, where he happily cradled her.

"Why what? Hey, Chance."

"Hey, Jolee. I was just asking Ford to help me gather some information about Keeley's father's business. Something seems fishy."

Jolee studied me for a minute, her pretty unmade-up face tilting to the side.

"You seem pretty interested in your new roommate. The same one that caused an outburst on Sunday."

Thankfully the barista called out Jolee's name, echoing in the room that her drink was ready and she skipped away.

"Don't worry about her. I'll help you," Ford said as he pulled out his phone.

"It's called Fox Trading, but I couldn't find anything on my way over here. I have a bad feeling. Also, they are her guardians, not her biological parents. See if you can find out anything."

Ford nodded as he typed away on his phone. "We're getting married."

"Thanks, man. Wait, what did you say?"

"I asked Jolee to marry me and she said yes. You can wipe that smirk off your face. I'm just as surprised as you. Jesus Christ, man, I want to have a family with that woman. She's everything."

"I'm happy for you, Ford." I was holding back my laugh at the conflicted expression he had on his face until Jolee arrived and I burst out laughing.

"You don't have to look so miserable about it," she said in a joking manner as I exploded in laughter. The couple at the table in the corner opted to leave the coffee shop. My brother wrapped his fiancée in his arms and placed a kiss on her lips.

"Congratulations," I said to the happy couple as they embraced on the single chair while I continued to chuckle.

Jolee's cup of warm drink sat in her hand while Ford nuzzled her neck. I wondered if they remembered that they were out in public, but then I didn't seem to care when I was with Keeley either.

"I'm headed out," I told them as I stood from my seat. "I'm thrilled to have you as a sister, Jolee." Leaning down, I placed a gentle kiss on her cheek before I left the coffee shop.

Glancing up and down the sidewalk, I considered heading to the college bar across the street, but that just wasn't what I wanted for the evening. Instead, I called up my tattoo artist to see if he had an opening for the evening. There was no design in mind, but the pain of the needle piercing the skin would be a welcome distraction.

The shop had a visiting artist, Cliff from some small town in North Carolina named Carson, and I was hesitant to let him tattoo me, but when he introduced himself, I knew I had nothing to worry about. He was in town for a tattoo convention where he received some award. I had a back piece I had been adding random designs to and allowed Cliff to do what he pleased; I was there for the adrenaline rush after all.

Amanda, who worked as the front desk receptionist, sat on the stool by the table where I was being worked on. She had been trailing her finger up and down my arm while Cliff worked his magic.

She was making idle small talk, but I had little interest in the conversation or more, which surprised me the most. All I could think about was Keeley sitting on the couch, miserable and confused at how I acted. And, fuck, I was so used to being an asshole that caring about someone's feelings was completely foreign.

"Hey, Cliff?" I asked as he outlined the two turtledoves to represent Tracy and my favorite Christmas movie, *Home Alone 2*.

"Yeah," the ex-military soldier grunted.

"What do you do when the girl you hated, maybe now you don't hate so much?"

Amanda chose that moment to sink her long purple-tipped claws into my arm as if she had some sort of claim on me.

"Well, Chance, I've been in that position. Just stick around. She'll come to you when she needs you and then she'll realize that you've been there all along."

"I'm not sure that will work with this one."

"How long have you two been going at it?"

I resisted the urge to sit up and snarl at Cliff. "We haven't been fucking! We were just. . .disagreeing about our living situation."

"Mmhmm," he replied. "Take it from me; if you're not serious about her, just keep it in your pants, eh?"

"You can relieve yourself with me," Amanda replied, leaning toward me.

"Not interested," I grunted. The platinum blonde, pierced beauty stormed off at my admission, leaving a chuckling Cliff in her wake.

"It will work out if it's meant to," Cliff added as he finished the shading of the birds. "You're all set."

Sitting up, I allowed him to cover the piece before I pulled my shirt over my head. "Thanks, man."

"Anytime. I'd say head up front so Amanda can check you out, but I think I'll handle it this time."

"I appreciate that."

Following Cliff to the front, I handed him my credit card, where he completed the transaction and sent me on my way.

The lights were off in the apartment when I opened the door except for a small lamp Keeley had placed on a little table in the entry area. She had only been here for a handful of days, but she had already started to leave her mark on the place.

Classes started the next day and I knew I needed to get things ready for the early morning practice. I wondered if Keeley would come through and help me keep up with my school work as she agreed.

I planned on making some dinner and walked down the hall to see if my roommate was around. Her door was closed, but there was a light shining underneath. A normal person would knock on her door and wait for her to answer, but I wasn't anywhere close to normal.

Turning the knob, I barged into the room. Keeley responded with a shriek and papers flying through the air.

"Stop doing that!" she cried out as she stood from her bed and started picking up the papers. A few fell at my feet and I picked them up, reading the delicate handwriting.

"What are these?" I asked her as I looked up to find Keeley leaning down with her perfect round ass in the air. My mouth salivated at the thought of walking over and sinking my teeth in the warm flesh. Fuck, I shouldn't have walked into her room.

From upside down, she mumbled, "Notes for the advice and confession boxes around campus. I've been writing and sorting some to deliver tomorrow."

"What about the ones people drop in?"

"I'll collect them once a week and take them to Colleen with the paper. She has someone that runs an advice piece in the school paper. She will answer them anonymously. It's sort of a social experiment that Colleen is running."

Handing her the small stack I collected, I sat on the edge of her bed as she placed them with another stack. "How did you get involved with all of this?"

Shrugging her shoulders, Keeley responded as she sat next to me. "I answered an ad in the school paper. Looking for something to do, I guess. Maybe it would give me a chance to learn that I'm not the only one unhappy with the way my life was going."

"You know it's not hard to change the path."

"It is when your father pays your tuition. That's why I didn't want Link to tell my father that I had no place to live. My father would bring me home quicker than I could have packed my things.

"Anyway, can I help you with something?"

"I was going to make some pasta for dinner. I wasn't sure if you wanted to join me."

"For someone that didn't want me to live here, you've shared two meals and a movie with me."

I joined her giggle with my laughter. She wasn't wrong. Since our bathroom moment, I couldn't seem to shake my need for her.

"Maybe I'm trying new things just like my roommate."

Keeley twisted her body to face me, her eyes darting back and forth as she stares at me.

"Okay. I'd like to join you," Keeley finally said.

"Want to help me knock another item off your list?" I asked while standing.

"I think I'll stick to one at a time for now. And I should probably start with something a little easier than homemade pasta. I was thinking macaroni and cheese out of a box."

"Suit yourself. I'll let you know when it's ready."

As I was slicing the ravioli pasta, Keeley made her way out of the room and took a seat at the kitchen counter to watch, but neither of us spoke. Except, the silence wasn't uncomfortable. Being in her presence relaxed me in a way that no one else could.

Stirring the sauce, I lifted the wooden spoon and held it out for Keeley to taste. Her resounding moan caused my dick to jump in my pants. She licked her lips and I was about to ignore dinner and take her back to my bedroom. Those plump pillows would look delectable wrapped around my cock.

"That's delicious, Chance. Where did you learn to cook like that?"

Involuntarily I flinched at the question and I wondered if she noticed. I should have known that she would be curious about my culinary skills. College-aged guys weren't known for their epicurean abilities.

But I knew if I told her just enough of where I learned it, she would want to know more.

"I, uh, learned from Tracy. I was a hungry kid," I fibbed and I hated how easily it came. Here I was hoping that Keeley would choose to ask me on a date to a baseball game and I lied to her like it was nothing.

"I bet she was so great. My parents never taught me how to do anything but math."

Damn, now I even felt bad.

"Shit, that was a lie." I turned to face her and witnessed her eyes widen in surprise.

"Tracy didn't teach you?"

"No, she did, but it was one of the few things my mom, my real mom, taught me when I was little. I could poach an egg by the time I was three."

Keeley reached out a soft hand and covered mine with it. Her reaction wasn't what I expected. She was wearing a smile; the small gentle kind that let you know they were appreciative.

"Thank you for telling me. I bet it's hard to open up about your past sometimes."

"You have no idea." The smile grew on my face before I could stop it and despite my surly reputation, I didn't hate it.

RENEE HARLESS

CHAPTER NINE

KEELEY

Chance had acted differently since he offered to get me tickets to a Red Sox game that was happening the following weekend. Originally I had wanted to ask him to be my date, but my fear got the best of me. The embarrassment of being turned down by a Ridge Rogue that I lived with would be too much to take, and awkward, to say the least. Instead, I'd been on the search for someone tolerable to take to the game. Jolee and Sarah had tried to help, but they didn't realize that I had zero desire to find someone. It was just a means to check a box off my list.

Walking around campus, I was pleased to see a couple of different students grabbing the confession boxes' positive messages spread across the campus. At first, I thought Colleen was nuts to put something like that in place. Almost everyone at Wellington Ridge University was so far into themselves that they would never confess their secrets to a stranger; they'd rather pay thousands of dollars to the onsite therapist.

The first advice column for this semester was going to be published on Friday and I was interested to see what the students had to say. It was tempting to ask for my own piece of advice regarding Chance and the bucket list. Would they tell me to go for it or ignore the pull that I had toward him? What about my father? Would the advice editor tell me that I should live my own life or continue on the path of a stable and secure job?

I had no idea that living with Chance would have me questioning everything.

Walking toward the library, I got flashes of my time hiding in the stacks when I was homeless. That time felt so long ago but was only a week and a half. As I walked inside, I feared that a security guard was waiting to take me away; somehow, they'd found out that I had been sleeping there.

Making my way to the third floor that I frequented so often, I found a table not far from the secret door I'd discovered. I was still curious about when it was used last.

The college was established in the 1980s, not too old, but it had functioned as a boarding school before then. The secrets these walls could tell.

"Hey," a deep voice called out as I was busy emptying my backpack. I looked up and found a good-looking guy I recognized. He lived across the hall from Link. We'd said hello a few times in the stairwell and at the mailboxes, but I didn't know his name or anything else.

"Hi. You live in the same apartment complex as me, right?" I asked as I finished setting out the material I needed to go over with Chance.

"Yeah. I'm Kyle," he said, holding out his hand. I glanced down and noticed how well-manicured and soft it looked compared to the rough and callused palm and fingers of Chance's.

"Keeley. It's nice to meet you. . .officially."

"You too. So, are you. . .um. . .living with the Ridge Rogue? I've seen you leave his place a few times." Kyle blushed, but it seemed insincere. Like he could just turn on the bashfulness and charm on a whim.

"I'm living there for now. I needed a temporary place to stay and Chance was helping me out."

"Cool. Do you think you'd want to go grab dinner or something one night?"

This was it. This was the opportunity to check an item off my list. Kyle wasn't the man for me, but he was cute and I'm sure we'd have a few things to talk about at the game. It would be awkward seeing him around the complex, but that was something I'd have to deal with.

"What do you think about baseball?"

Chance came strutting down the main walkway an hour later with a gaggle of blonde beauties trailing behind him. Today was his first open practice on campus, where students could sit in the stands and watch. The university had some weird fixation with putting their sports players on display. Even the debate and chess team were allowed onlookers.

He brushed the women off and they scattered as he took a seat at the table I had reserved. Glancing up from my class notes, I spotted the tell-tale signs of lack of sleep on Chance. He looked exhausted.

"Chance, are you okay? You look tired."

Rubbing a hand down his face, Chance let his workout bag drop from his shoulder with a thud and he slouched against the table.

"I haven't been getting much sleep."

"Anything I can do to help?"

Chance's eyes connected with mine and held for a moment. He was silently telling me something that I couldn't decipher. I was too lost in the green irises to understand the silent message.

"Not right now."

"Okay. Want to start with your political science class?" I asked Chance as he pulled out his notebook from his bag.

We worked for another hour on his current classes. With every session we had together, I was impressed with how smart Chance was. He didn't need my help, but I understood his desire to have a tutor; most athletes did. We agreed that we would only work together at the library to keep an invisible line drawn on our roommate agreement.

"I think you're going to do great this semester, Chance. You've already got a good handle on all of the material."

Reaching out, Chance tucked a piece of hair that fell from my ponytail behind my ear. His finger lingered on my earlobe. I silently wished he would slide his hand into my hair and pull me toward his mouth.

"Um. . .so, I checked off a box on my list," I said half-heartedly.

Chance's fingers dropped from my skin as if it burned him. I was startled at the loss of contact.

"What?" Chance sounded angry, but for the life of me, I didn't know why.

"Kyle. He lives across the hall from you and Link. I asked him on a date to the Red Sox game. What do you think?"

If someone could physically turn into the Incredible Hulk, I would believe that Chance was undergoing that transformation. His skin turned pasty white instead of green as if he was ill, and his eyes grew dim.

"Chance?" I called out his name as he stood from the table. He ran a hand through his hair as his chest heaved with jarring breaths. He seemed to be fighting a battle and losing. "Chance, are you okay?"

"No," he growled as he approached me, hauling me from my chair until I was pressed against his chest, my feet dangling in the air. "I can't concentrate when all I can think about is tasting your pussy again. I want to feel your juices drip down my chin when you explode on my face."

"Chance," I moaned, my panties growing wet as I imagined him following through with his cravings.

Setting me down, he kept one arm wrapped around my waist while his other hand skimmed across my hips to the button on my denim shorts. He unfastened the closure with the ease of an expert then slid down the zipper.

"Chance," I whispered as both a threat and in surprise. We weren't alone in the library. Though this floor was the least used, a handful of graduate students were still studying at tables just down the hall. "Someone could see us."

"Let them." His hand dove beneath the elastic band of my panties and pressed against my sex.

"Chance, we can't," I half-heartedly pleaded as he slipped a finger inside my channel.

"I will have your pussy again, Keeley. Right now. You're fucking soaked. Don't deny what we both know you want."

"But. . .I. . . there is a place," I said breathlessly, immediately missing the feel of his fingers as he pulled his hand free. At first, I thought he would put an end to whatever thing he had started, but as Chance stuck his finger in his mouth, savoring the flavor, I knew that he wasn't going to back out.

A smarter girl would have knocked some sense back into herself, but I never claimed to be intelligent. My body was already addicted to the things that Chance could make me feel even after one tryst, and there was no way that I was going to deny myself that feeling.

Grabbing his wrist, I guided him down the stacks of books until I came to the window I had come to know so well. Blindly I searched for the button as Chance grabbed my breast from behind, placing his lips on the side of my neck.

The sound of the door's mechanics reverberated around us and Chance pulled away.

"Well, damn." As he stepped back from me and inspected the space, his voice was filled with awe. "We're going to discuss how you found this later. Right now, I'm hungry." Chance grabbed a fistful of my shirt and tugged me forward until we were both inside the space. There was just enough room for the both of us to move around comfortably once I joined him inside.

Taking a step closer, Chance cupped his hand around my jaw as he commanded, "Close the door, Keeley."

"There's no light in here."

"I don't need any light to set you off."

Extending my arm, I touched the wall until I found the button and pressed it. The door took it's time closing, and as the light from the room began to disappear, I was able to snag a glimpse of the predatory devilish grin growing on Chance's face.

I'd expected him to release my jaw as soon as we were bathed in darkness, but his fingers tightened instead. Anyone else would have been scared, but I was so turned on that I was about to melt into a puddle at his feet.

"Let me be very clear, little mouse," Chance said as he brushed his mouth across mine then roughly nibbled on my bottom up. "These lips are mine. Your pussy is mine. And your orgasms are mine. Do you understand?" he asked as his hand plunged back inside my panties. "Do you understand, Keeley?"

His breath swept across my cheek and I shivered. I wasn't sure what he was implying because we both knew that Chance wasn't staking a claim as a boyfriend, but I said, "Yes."

His mouth slammed against mine and I wondered how long it had been since Chance had kissed someone. His kiss was eager and possessive as he held my chin, tiling my head where he wanted me. At the same time, he thrust two fingers deep in my channel, his tongue mimicking the motion as he begged for entrance between my lips.

Fuck, the man could kiss. I could easily stay locked in this room with him until we were more than sated.

A whimper escaped as he pulled his mouth away and released my jaw. A moan of excitement replaced it as he pushed me back against the stone wall. My shorts were tossed aside and Chance's fingers glided along my hips as he played with the elastic of my panties. The soft cotton quickly joined my shorts on the floor by my feet.

Lifting my leg onto his shoulder, Chance sealed his mouth onto my sex.

My head knocked against the wall as I took in the sensations that flowed through me. God, he was masterful with that tongue of his and I was edging toward my release faster than I had wanted, but there was no use in holding it back.

"Chance, don't stop," I bellowed as my hand fisted in his hair.

In the shadow-filled room, explosions of light surrounded me as I plunged over the edge in my release. It was so powerful and overwhelming that I felt my knees begin to buckle in exhaustion, but Chance's strong arms cradled me.

He kissed me again, my flavor lingering on his tongue. It wasn't as unpleasant as I had expected and I returned his kiss with eagerness.

Boldly I reached out and ran my hand across the front of his shorts, cupping his erection. It thrilled me to know that I had that effect on him.

"Take my cock out. I want to feel your hand slide on my shaft."

I quickly complied and grinned against his lips as he groaned into my mouth when I felt the weight of his dick in my palm. He was large, I knew this from his naked introduction, but Chance was gloriously endowed at full mast. My thumb ran over the piercing at the tip of his cock and he answered by shifting his hips.

Selfishly I wanted to own this piece of him as he owned me, but Chance was not one to give that kind of control to someone.

I ran my hand up and down on his cock, amazed as he continued to grow in my hold.

"You're driving me mad, little mouse."

"Maybe we should all be a little wild," I replied. I felt wanton and gathered his shirt, lifting it on his chest. Chance quickly finished the task and repeated the move with my shirt and bra.

I was standing naked in front of the most ridiculously attractive man I had ever met, and I couldn't even see him. Good thing I had a wonderful memory.

Something came over me as I continued to pump his shaft and he cupped my breasts. I wanted more, needed it more than I needed my vision.

Taking a small step closer to him, I hitched my leg around his waist. Holding all the power in my hand, I stood on my toes and shifted my hips so that I could run the tip of his cock against my soaked pussy.

"Oh, fuck," he growled as I repeated the motion. "Keeley, you're playing with fire."

"I know. I'm not scared to be burned."

His voice was tight and controlled as I continued to rock my hips against his erection. "I don't have any condoms."

"I'm on the pill. I want you to fuck me, Chance. I want to own your cock."

Powerfully Chance spun me around so that my body was pressed against the cold wall.

"No one owns me, little mouse. I'll take what I want when I want it," he explained as he whispered against my ear, pulling my hips toward him. His fingers dug into my skin and I relished in the pinch of pain. "And right now, I want to feel your hot pussy squeeze my cock. Is that what you want?"

"Yes," I immediately replied.

I felt a nudge from behind. His cock slapped against my ass before slipping between my legs. He glided the velvety skin against my drenched folds and my body quaked, yearning for more.

"My little mouse is greedy, isn't she? She wants to feel me push my cock deep inside her sex."

"Yes, please." I was begging him for more. "I want it all."

His fingertips traveled up my back, following my spine, then caressed the skin across my shoulder before wrapping his hand around my neck. The sex I'd experienced before had been plain and vanilla. Thomas never allowed me anywhere but in bed and on my back. I'd pleaded with him to try something new, but he was set in his boring ways.

As Chance plunged his cock into my sex, I knew that this was going to be anything but boring.

"God, you're tight. Fuck," he said, sliding out then thrusting back in. The thick shaft stretched me as he pushed to the hilt. His fingers tightened around my neck as he held our bodies in place.

Nibbling at my ear, Chance asked, "Are you ready?"

"Yes."

Chance pushed at my shoulder with a forceful hand until I bent forward at the hips. It traveled down my spine, and then he smacked my ass as he pushed his cock inside my core.

"Oh!" I cried out, but it wasn't in pain. I felt waves of pleasure at the ache he left behind.

"You like your ass smacked, mouse? Your pussy is clenching around my cock right now."

"Yes, more," I begged as he continued to pound into me. One of his hands reached forward and cupped my breast, pinching the sensitive nipple. I closed my eyes to savor the pleasure coursing through me even though we were in darkness.

The only sounds in the small space were our heavy breathing, moans of pleasure, and the sound of our wet skin slapping together.

Suddenly Chance withdrew himself from my sex and I whimpered at the loss. I was spun around and lifted in the air, my legs automatically wrapping around Chance's waist. My nipples brushed against the small smattering of hair on his chest as he pushed my back against the wall.

I was surprised when Chance pressed his mouth against mine as he guided his cock back into my pussy. I hadn't anticipated the intimate gesture, but I could quickly become obsessed with his kiss.

Chance took control of my hips, plunging into me over and over again. I rocked up and down, imitating his moves until our moans sang out in the room.

"Don't stop, Chance," I cried out as I wrapped my arms around his shoulders and buried my face against his neck. There were too many sensations and I was becoming overwhelmed, but I still wanted more. I wanted to feel everything.

"Fuck, I'm going to come. I want to come in you, mouse. I want to know that I'm sliding out of your used-up pussy."

"Oh, god."

"Let me come in you."

"Yes. Oh, god. Yes!" I screamed as I came apart. Chance continued to hold me up as he drove himself into me over and over. He reached his precipice and groaned as he released himself inside my channel.

"Damn," he murmured as he slipped out and relaxed against me.

Quietly we stood in the black-filled hidden room that smelled of sweat and sex. The moment the chime of a mobile phone filled the space, Chance's demeanor changed. He stepped away from me and then suddenly the room was bathed in the bright white light of the flashlight on his phone. I blinked at the intrusion.

"Grab your clothes," he said nonchalantly, like he hadn't just given me an experience that I had only dreamed about. His pants were still around his ankles and he tugged them up as I reached for my panties and shorts near his feet.

I barely had my bra clasped when he started rooting around for the button that opened the door. Once he pressed it the door began sliding open and I frantically pulled my shirt over my head.

"Geez, Chance. Couldn't wait for me to finish getting dressed?"

Of course, the infuriating man only shrugged his shoulders as he stepped out of the room. I was left trailing behind him like the women from earlier.

I ignored the stares from a few of the students as I rushed behind him to get back to our table. Chance rocked the mussed-up look like it was his daily attire, but I probably looked like I had been caught in a hurricane.

By the time I caught up to Chance, he already had his bag slung over his shoulder and was typing away on his phone.

"Chance. . ." I said breathlessly.

"See you later," he replied without a backward glance and headed toward the stairwell.

I should have realized that this wasn't going to mean anything to Chance. It didn't really mean much to me other than getting to do something completely crazy. But he didn't have to treat me so indifferently like I was just any other girl.

But if he wanted me to forget that any of this happened, well, I had no problem with that. I had a date to plan and more items on my bucket list to check off.

CHAPTER TEN

CHANCE

Was I a dick for leaving Keeley in the library after having probably the best sex of my life? Yep. Would I have changed it? Not at all.

She didn't need to get attached to me. I would only bring her down. And my secrets were too big for her. Keeley didn't deserve to live in the shadows as I did.

Plus, I was never very good at putting other people first. That's why when our rendezvous ended and I had a message from Ford, I knew I needed to get out of that confined space where the scent of Keeley overwhelmed me.

He'd used a private investigator to track down information regarding Keeley's father and wanted to meet up at a bar the next town over. Drinking was the last thing I wanted to do. I'd rather find my roommate and convince her for round two. This would be the first time I ever wanted a second round with a woman.

Entering the bar, I immediately noticed Ford sitting on a stool with his attention focused on the flat screen in the corner where a football game was taking place. A woman sat on his other side trying to gain his interest, but he wasn't paying her any mind.

"Hey, man," I said as I clamped my hand on his shoulder. Ford's head swung around and there was an immediate sense of relief in his gaze.

"Hey. Let's go grab a table." Ford's eyes darted to the woman who was eyeing me up and down with interest.

We found a booth across from the bar and sat down, a server stopped by and we each ordered a beer.

"So, what did you find?" I started as the server stepped away.

Ford answered with a chuckle. "You realize your shirt is inside out, right?"

Glancing down at the material, I realized that he was right. The shirt was both inside out and backward.

"Yeah, I rushed out of the locker room. Sorry." The lie flowed easily and Ford didn't seem to notice.

As the server returned with our drinks, Ford pulled out a piece of paper from his pants pocket.

"So, from what we could gather, Fox Trading is a front company. As in, it is just a name. We're still trying to figure out what company actually controls it."

"That's it?"

"Not all of it. Interestingly, Fox Trading has been investigated twelve times in the last three years for falsifying records and tax evasion. And Mr. Fox has been arrested twice for drug possession, but all of the charges have been dropped."

"So, really, we know nothing more."

I was frustrated. Something didn't add up with Keeley's father and his business, but I had no proof of anything. I was sure there was something illegal going on.

"We're still digging into records, but I agree with you; something doesn't add up. And to top it off, there were no employee records. Not a single one. Now, why would someone leave their daughter in charge of a company without any reports or papers?"

"I agree. And she doesn't seem fazed about it at all. I keep trying to talk her out of taking the position, but she won't listen to me."

"Blood is a powerful way to convince someone to do something."

Something felt wrong about invading Keeley's private life, but I couldn't help myself. I needed answers, not just for me but for her. She didn't need to go into this life planned out for her blindly.

"Chance, why are you so concerned with this? What's in it for you?"

I chose that moment to drink half of my beer in one gulp before looking at my brother.

"I just. . .what would you do, Ford? If you knew someone was being forced into their future without a say, wouldn't you step in? Something just doesn't seem right about any of it."

"I get it. It's just maybe you're butting into something that could make things even worse. Have you thought about that?"

"If that's the case I'll do what I can to help her."

Ford started laughing. Not just a chuckle but an overzealous belly laugh that had patrons from all over the bar looking in our direction. Ford laughing wasn't something I was accustomed to. He spent most of his days before Jolee as a brooding asshole.

"What's so funny?"

"Never thought you would fall, man. You have it bad for Keeley."

"I don't have anything for her except for annoyance. She is stubborn and unwilling to listen to reason."

"Whatever you say." Ford finished up his beer and chucked a few dollars on the table. "Look, I'll have the PI keep digging. I agree that something doesn't seem right, but, man, you can't tell someone how to live their life. If she wants to follow her father's path, then she can."

"Thanks, Ford. I'm hoping to take her to a Red Sox game next weekend. Let me know if you and Jolee want to come."

"We're working with the shelter that weekend, but let's take a rain check."

I watched Ford leave while I chugged the last of my beer. The desire to get home to the apartment was strong, even if I knew that she would snarl at me the entire time.

It was deja vu walking into the darkened apartment. The light billowed out beneath the door of Keeley's room, but I couldn't bring myself to barge in there this time. Not that I wanted to give her privacy, but I didn't want to lead her on anymore than I had.

We'd crossed an invisible line and there was no going back. The easiest thing would be to try and ignore the earth-shattering sex we'd had and go back to fighting. I just wasn't sure that I could look at Keeley without my cock standing at attention.

I stepped into the kitchen to grab a bottle of water just as Keeley walked out of her bedroom. She had on the tiny boxer shorts that showed off her incredible legs and an oversized T-shirt with a neck opening that hung over her shoulder. My lips had touched that shoulder, had left my mark on her skin.

Silently she walked into the kitchen and I stepped aside as she opened the fridge door and grabbed a bottle of water for herself. Her hair was wet and twisted up on top of her head and I wanted nothing more than to tug the tie loose and let the strands fall down her back. Twisting off the cap, Keeley put the bottle to her lips and drank the entire thing at once. She slowly pulled the bottle down and locked eyes with me when she finished.

I wasn't sure what to say to rectify the mess I had caused. But I also knew that it was how things would have to be.

Swallowing the lump in my throat, I said, "Hey." I didn't recognize my voice.

"I ran into Kyle on the way back. He's excited about the baseball game. That is if you still plan on following through with the tickets."

Did I want to think about her going out with another guy after I had just fucked her? No. Did I realize that my jealousy was the main reason I needed to have her and claim her pussy? Also, yes. Did I care? No.

"So, you're still going with him after today?" I growled.

"Why wouldn't I? With the way you ended things, I was pretty certain that the decision was made for me."

The bottle crinkled in my hand as my fingers tightened. Keeley stared at my knuckles and I wondered if she remembered how my hand held her neck a few hours ago.

"You think he's going to fuck you as good as I did?" My lip lifted in a snarl as I imaged some pasty nerd trying to seduce my little mouse.

"No, Chance. I don't. It's just a date. One that was on my bucket list and now I can check off. He's a means to an end. I have zero desire to have sex with him."

"You don't, but I can guarantee that he does." I took a menacing step toward her, lowering my voice as I went. "I bet he's already pictured the twenty different ways he wants to take you with his minuscule pecker. In his mind, you'd be calling out his name as he tried to fuck you. But in reality, you'd be calling out my name. Know why, little mouse?"

"Why?" she replied breathlessly, her cheeks growing in redness as I spoke.

"Because your pussy is mine."

Thoughtlessly I reached out to touch her, but Keeley took a step back, then another as my hand dropped back to my side.

"You wield your asshole behavior around like it's the only thing you are, Chance. But you could be so much more than that if you let yourself."

"What you see is what you get, Keeley."

"That makes me sad for you. It must be miserable to know that your sole purpose is to ruin everyone you meet."

She spun on her heels and headed back toward her room, leaving me in her wake. Her words should have hurt, should have driven a knife deep within my heart. But my heart was a black mass that pumped my inky blood through my body and the only thing I felt was a desire for this girl that saw more of me than I liked.

Damn, now my cock was tenting my shorts at the thought of shoving it in her mouth the next time she argued with me.

After our single affair, I was surprised that Keeley never attempted to move out of the apartment. She gave me another envelope of rent money at my study session yesterday. Keeley seemed to ignore everything that had happened with us and went about her time as if we were random roommates. And it irritated the fuck out of me. It wasn't that I wanted her to follow me around like the other women I took to bed, but she seemed to have lost all interest, even in a friendship.

We'd gone back to ignoring each other in the apartment, not even sharing meals. It was like we were strangers.

The day of the Red Sox game came and I made sure to go through on my promise, with a catch. I had four tickets to the game, and I planned to tag along with my own date. I'd asked a girl that sat next to me in economics. She was one of the few that had zero interest in me but was a Red Sox fan. I offered her my extra ticket for a few weeks of homework. She also knew that this was not a date, but I needed to keep an eye on my naïve roommate.

"What time is Kyle picking you up?" I asked from the living room as I watched a cheesy reality show on television. She had no idea I planned on going to the game. I thought it best to keep her in the dark.

"He's not," Keeley replied as she stepped into the room. She had on frayed denim cutoffs that showcased her legs, my favorite feature, and a plaid red and blue shirt tied at her waist. She looked a little bit country and a whole lot of sexy as fuck. Damn, I wanted to bend her over the couch and help her remember who she belongs to.

Then her words registered. "What? Say that again."

Rolling her eyes, Keeley said, "He's not picking me up. I told him to meet me there."

"How'd you plan on getting there?"

"The bus."

I grunted at her response. I could offer to drive her, but it would be tight in the backseat since I had to pick up Darla. But I wasn't sure the bus was the safest route for her to take. She was a grown woman, though I knew she would do the complete opposite of what I told her.

With her tickets in hand, I watched her leave the apartment and it took everything in me to keep from following her to Fenway Park. I only wanted her to be safe and I wasn't sure a cute girl like Keeley would ever be safe.

After changing into a navy-blue Henley T-shirt, I left the apartment and picked Darla up at the coffee shop where she worked. She was overly enthusiastic in the car, thanking me numerous times for the invite. Darla promised her girlfriend that she'd grab a souvenir while we were there.

I considered not telling Darla about Keeley or the situation she was about to be thrust upon. Darla didn't need to go in blindsided where the tension would be high. Luckily, Darla didn't seem to mind and was intrigued. So, in a move that I couldn't have predicated, I gave her the full sordid details of my short but convoluted situation with Keeley. I had to catch myself from telling her about both Keeley's and my past, but I didn't want to weigh her down with all of that hell.

Finally, we arrived in the city and I searched around for parking, lucking out to find some street parking about two blocks from the entrance of Fenway. Darla seemed to be ecstatic and since we were early, we went ahead and searched for a coveted souvenir for her to take home.

We grabbed a couple of beers and made our way to our seats between home plate and third base, six rows back. Keeley and Kyle hadn't arrived yet and I was almost gleeful in my anticipation of her expression when she saw me sitting there. Tormenting her was becoming one of my favorite pastimes.

While Darla was busy taking pictures, I scrolled through some social media on my phone, landing on Keeley's profile via Jolee's. She didn't post often, but she had a lot of pictures of her with Sarah, Jolee, Haley, and Jolee's cousin Willow who used to attend Wellington University. There was definitely a difference between her and her friends; though she looked happy, it appeared forced. Like Keeley knew her freedom was on a timeline.

A message from Ford popped up on my phone saying that he had some more information and to call him immediately. With my phone in hand, I stood up, only to find Keeley glaring at me from the entrance to our row.

"I should have known," she said with a snarl. Her arms were crossed against her chest in anger, which only pushed up her magnificent breasts that Kyle also seemed to take notice of. He looked just as I predicted – douchebag with daddy's trust fund. I wondered if his biceps would break through the too-small polo shirt that he was wearing.

"Hey, I'm Kyle. I live across the hall from you," he said with his hand extended in an introduction.

To show Keeley that I could be a little more than an asshole, I shook his hand and introduced Darla. I almost laughed at the double-take both he and Keeley made. Darla had smooth dark skin and she wore an easy smile. And in combination with her heavy Southern accent, she immediately put everyone at ease. At first glance, it would be hard-pressed for anyone to realize that Darla swung for the other team. She only disclosed that information when it mattered. And I had a feeling she was getting pleasure out of watching Keeley try to figure out if she and I were on a date.

Yeah, Darla may be my new best friend.

Kyle brushed past me to get to his seat and then Keeley followed. I didn't miss the opportunity to let my hand trail across her bottom as she went. She didn't even respond, but Kyle's eyes narrowed at my hand.

I kept up a conversation with Darla until the game started, trying to listen in to Keeley's as well. I wasn't going to call Ford until later, but I asked that he send me whatever he found out. Unfortunately, I couldn't open those messages with Keeley sitting beside me.

About halfway through the game, I asked Darla if she wanted a Fenway hotdog and she eagerly agreed. Biting my tongue, I looked over and asked Kyle, who was sitting far too close to Keeley, if they wanted one as well.

"Naw, I don't eat hotdogs. They're terrible for you," Keeley's date said as he reached behind her and rested his arm on the back of the stadium seat, rubbing his fingers on the bare skin of her shoulder. Within my mouth, I ground my teeth together. He was touching what was mine.

"Keeley?" I asked, but Kyle spoke up, "We're good. Thanks."

Her eyes lit up when I asked. Her blue eyes darted between the two of us and I waited for her to explode on him the same way she would have if I had spoken for her. I mean, I knew she wanted the freaking hotdog. But her asshole date thought he could speak for her.

Except Keeley remained silent, tucking her chin toward her chest.

"Suit yourself," I told them as I shuffled out of the row, winking at Darla on the way because I knew she could handle herself.

While waiting in line, I read through Ford's screenshots from his investigator. He found ties to Ford's father, Senator Hastings, and connections to a vast drug cartel in Mexico. He wanted to meet with me to hand over the information personally.

Fifteen minutes later, and with some new knowledge from Ford's texts, I returned to my seat with six of the salty goodies that were Fenway hotdogs. Kyle rolled his eyes and huffed as I handed out two hotdogs to Darla and settled the others on my lap. Keeley glanced down at the food and then turned her attention back to the game. Kyle's feminine-like hand continued to rub circles on Keeley's shoulder, and I wanted to rip it off. Instead, I tore into the wiener, devouring half of it in one bite.

There was a small break in the game and Kyle chose that moment to exit the row. I assumed to head to the bathroom as he complained that there wasn't anything he would dare eat at the stadium.

Stuck-up prick.

The moment he was out of sight, I handed the two hotdogs I had left to Keeley. Her eyes lit up as I placed them on her lap.

"Thank you. Oh my gosh, I'm starving. He wanted to go get sushi later, but I really wanted one of these hotdogs."

"You're welcome."

As she ate, I gave her a proper introduction to Darla and the two of them hit it off, as I knew would happen. By the time Kyle returned, Keeley was occupying my seat while I swapped for hers.

"You know," Kyle whispered next to me as he begrudgingly took his seat, clearly unhappy with the seat change, "don't wait up for her to come home tonight."

"Why is that?" I asked through gritted teeth.

"Because she's coming home with me."

CHAPTER ELEVEN

KEELEY

Darla was one of those people that could suck you into a conversation and then suddenly five hours passed as if it was five minutes. I was completely in love with her and her enthusiasm for life. She also had a bucket list like mine, though hers was more about doing extreme things like bungee jumping or spelunking.

At first, I had been so filled with jealousy at the beautiful woman that sat next to Chance in the stadium. Then she showed me pictures of her and her girlfriend on her phone when she had the first opportunity and that jealousy had melted away.

But even though I was lost in her Red Sox knowledge, I could feel Chance tense beside me. He gave off this energy that I could feel wherever we went. Even if I was sitting in my bedroom, I knew when he entered the apartment building. It was something that I couldn't explain, but everything inside me shifted when he was near.

I turned in my seat to see Chance stiffen.

"Excuse me? What did you say?" Chance questioned.

"Calm down, man," Kyle said with a forced chuckle, but Chance wasn't backing down, even as I placed my hand on his arm.

"Chance," I whispered, but I knew the red was seeping into his vision.

"Say it again," Chance threatened with his hands balling into fists. "Let her hear what you said."

Kyle's eyes darted over to me, then back to Chance. "I said that she was coming home with me. Don't make it a big deal, man."

Chance stood and leaned over Kyle. They were evenly matched in size, but the rage filling Chance would be his hindrance. "Keeley can make her own decisions, asshole. And if you so much as think that you have a shot at taking her to bed, I will end you myself."

"Is that a threat, Rogue?" Kyle sneered as he began to stand.

Chance didn't let him get to his full height. Instead, he leaned into my date's face as he fisted the collar of Kyle's polo shirt.

"It's a fucking promise. Keeley will never be yours. If you see her, me, or any of my brothers in the hall, I suggest you turn and go the other way. Do I make myself clear?"

"A Ridge Rogue standing up for a woman? She must have one hell of a golden pussy. . ." Kyle said before Chance pounced on him.

Everyone had told me that fights happened in slow motion, but I never believed them until now.

"Chance!" I shouted, my voice sounding filtered in my own ears.

Around us, beer and food splattered as people tried to duck out of the way from the flying fists, but I wasn't so lucky as Chance's elbow collided with my cheek. He began to turn and Kyle took his shot. I watched the blood pool out of Chance's nose and lip as Kyle threw a right jab, but then Chance countered with an uppercut and jab that had Kyle falling back onto the people in the seats next to him.

Somehow Darla managed to dive between the two guys and separate them, showing a strength I did not expect from her lithe figure.

"Oh my gosh, Chance, are you okay?" I cradled his head and upper body in my lap as Kyle stood, holding his hand to his head, bleeding rapidly.

"You're going to help him? What about me?" he cried out and the group around him groaned. Somewhere a few people called out that he deserved it.

Security showed up a second later and escorted us all out of the stadium, luckily not banning us from future games once Darla and I explained what had happened. I still thought Kyle should not have been allowed back, but I didn't make the rules.

Kyle ran off once we were escorted from our row and Darla stayed with us. Chance stayed quiet through the entire ordeal, but his eyes kept looking me over. I didn't need to glance down at him to feel his gaze on me.

"I'm sorry about this, Darla," I apologized. She had come for a good time and ended up leaving early due to two assholes misbehaving. She waved off my apology, saying that this was the most fun she'd had in forever.

"You okay to take him home?" she whispered to me as Chance stood off to the side with his head down with his fists clenching and then unclenching. He was battling his internal rage, and instead of fear, I felt sorry for him.

That was not a way to live your life.

"Yeah. Are you sure you don't want a ride? It's really okay."

"No, I'll take the bus. Maybe we can get together soon?"

"Yes, absolutely!"

Darla and I exchanged information and a hug before the bus arrived and she hopped up. Thank goodness Wellington had a private bus to take students back to the university. It worked like a ride share and would pick up students as needed.

"Hey," I said as I got closer to Chance who stood leaning against a no parking sign. "Are you ready?"

He didn't answer but nodded and pointed in the direction of where he parked.

I tried to make conversation as we walked, but I had given up by the time we approached the car. There was a cut on his cheek that continued to bleed from a stupid gold ring that Kyle was wearing on the pinky finger of his right hand.

Even when we arrived back at the apartment complex, Chance had remained silent. But as we got to our floor, his eyes landed on Kyle's door. His shoulders began to move up and down as he sucked in air.

"Come on," I said as I pushed him toward our apartment, hoping he could ignore Kyle's.

Luckily he stepped over our threshold and calmed down. I tossed his keys on the small table I'd placed in the little entryway, noticing how high the stack had become with mail for our previous tenant. I wasn't sure why Chance was keeping them, but maybe he planned on returning them to the postal service.

He tried to brush past me, but I reached out and grabbed his arm, halting his movements.

"Let me clean you up." I expected a protest, but he willingly let me lead him to the sofa, where he sat down with a thud. Quickly I rushed to the bathroom and grabbed the first aid kit, finding that Chance hadn't moved a muscle when I returned.

He sat with a demeaning scowl on his face and I couldn't tell if it was directed at himself or at me.

With a clean cloth and a bowl of hot water that I grabbed from the kitchen, I sat on the coffee table and began gently brushing away the dried-on blood.

"Did you want me to call Link?" I asked him if he'd prefer his brother to take over the task.

"No," he replied before flinching as I cleaned a particularly jagged cut.

"I'd say you may need stitches for this cut here on your cheek, but we can probably get by with some butterfly tape."

"I don't care."

With the cloth in hand, I continued to tend to his wounds, trying not to cry, knowing that my asshole of a date wore that stupid ring marring Chance's face. Luckily Kyle didn't look any better because Chance clearly had experience fighting.

While I placed antibiotic ointment on the cuts, I chose that moment to thank Chance for standing up for me. Even on rocky terrain, he still made sure that I was treated with respect. I wondered if he would have done the same for any of the other women he'd been with.

"It was nothing."

"It wasn't nothing," I said more forcefully, my eyes welling with unshed tears in the process. "You got hurt because of me. Because of a decision that I made."

"Keeley," he replied softly, his hand gently resting on my knee. My skin burned under his palm. He could fight it all he wanted, but there was a connection between us. Something more than physical; it was chemical. And overwhelming.

His hand fell from my knee as I stood, taking a small step closer to him. Chance's legs straddled mine as my shins brushed against the leather of the couch.

I said his name on a whisper, weaving my fingers through his hair. Chance slid his hands around the backs of my thighs, gliding them up until he reached the bottom of my ass beneath my shorts. I leaned forward as his fingers slipped under my panties and captured his lips with mine. He flinched from the cut on his lower lip but then returned the kiss more forcefully.

Slipping his hands free from my shorts, Chance placed them on my hips to guide me forward. I positioned my knees on either side of his hips, moving my hand down from his hair and wrapping it around his neck. I rocked myself against his growing erection and savored the way his fingers tightened on my waist.

He undid the knot at the bottom of my shirt with deft fingers and unfastened the buttons. My breasts were exposed to him behind the lace cups of my bra, but Chance didn't spare a second to glance down at the globes. He continued to control our kiss with a possession I had never known before.

"Chance, please," I murmured against his lips. How had I become so addicted to him? How could I crave him at the same time that I hated him? Except maybe I didn't hate him. Maybe I just didn't understand him.

"What do you need, little mouse?"

"I want you to take me to bed."

Pulling away, Chance moved his lips along my jawline and down my neck, nibbling and sucking along the way. He was leaving his mark on me and I didn't even care.

"I don't do romance, Keeley. I can't be that for you."

Romance was the last thing I wanted. What I needed was to feel the fullness and pleasure that I knew he could only give me.

"Then fuck me, Chance. Here and now. I need it," I told him as I rocked my hips into him again, certain that he could feel the heat of my core through our shorts.

With a quick twist, he had my back on the couch with his larger body hovering over mine. "Now, that I can do."

As expected, Chance and I ignored the growing attraction between us. After the sex on the couch post Red Sox game, I didn't see him for three days. When he finally stumbled into the apartment with bloodshot eyes and dark circles rimming the edges, his only explanation was that he was helping Tracy with something around her house.

Did I believe him? No, not at all. But I hadn't gone to anymore Sunday dinners since the first one, so I had to trust his word.

I may have also been a bit jealous and concerned that he had been occupying his time with another female instead of being at the apartment.

Of course, when I asked if that was the case and accused him of lying about helping Tracy, he blew up at me, claiming that it wasn't any of my business. And he was right. We weren't dating, nor did I have any claim on him.

I just needed to remind myself that we weren't exclusive. There was no saying where he was putting his cock because it wasn't with me.

"Ugh!" I growled in the kitchen as I pounded some chicken, trying to follow a recipe. One of my other bucket list items was to cook. More specifically, to follow a recipe and it was edible. I was one of those people that could burn water. My father never let me speak with the staff in our house, so I had no one that could teach me.

"What did that chicken ever do to you?" I startled at the voice and the meat pounder flung out of my hand toward the sound. I turned as Chance ducked out of the way and the metal tool slammed into a cabinet door. "Geez, give a guy a warning next time," he joked as he slid his practice bag off his shoulder.

"Talking to me now?" I asked as I placed the chicken in a baking dish. There was a bowl of seasoning I had put together and started sprinkling on top of the white meat.

"We'll see. What are you doing?"

"Cooking."

"Is that what you call it?"

"Well, I'm following the recipe I found. I wanted to check it off the list."

"Seems more like baking. I could have helped you; you know."

"Right. When would I have asked, Chance? When you weren't home, or when you were ignoring me? Oh, maybe when you were entertaining your fan club around campus? When would have been the best time?"

In obvious Chance fashion, he shrugged his shoulders and grabbed a sauté pan from a lower cabinet, brushing my hip with his own as he passed. He glanced at the seasonings I had laid out and gave a single nod before turning toward the refrigerator and grabbing some of his fresh vegetables.

"Stir fry, okay?"

He ignored my response and poured olive oil in the pan, then reached for a cutting board to slice up the chicken.

"Chance, are you going to answer me?"

"I'm just cooking dinner."

"Well, I had planned on cooking dinner. And since you're here, I figured you could tell me why you're keeping your distance."

With a knife in hand, Chance sliced the vegetables and then the chicken with a precision I had only seen on television cooking shows.

"You know why, Keeley."

"I really don't. And I needed to cook this meal to check it off my list, so once again, you controlled everything," I said as I dumped the rag I had tossed over my shoulder onto the counter.

"How about I show you?" he suggested and I rolled my eyes, turning my back to him.

"No thanks."

"Come on. I won't bite. I'll help you cook something easy."

"Honestly, Chance, I'm not sure I trust you to do anything. How about we just stick to tutoring and rent and call it a day?"

"I wish I could, but I promised I'd help you check off items from your list. So, get your cute butt in here and let me show you how to make some stir fry."

The infuriating man even pouted his bottom lip while he waited for my answer.

"Fine. Show me how to cook this meal properly and then just. . .leave me be."

"After we eat together."

"I didn't agree to that."

"That's all part of the cooking experience. To watch someone savor the flavors you created on their tongue."

Everything Chance said had some sort of sexual innuendo and I found myself nodding as I leaned my hip against the kitchen counter.

I followed Chance's direction as we cooked dinner alongside each other. He was a surprisingly good teacher, a slight turn of the table in our dynamic. Chance was patient and quick to adjust an error I had made without degradation. He consoled me when I accidentally flicked a piece of chicken off the pan. A memory of my father screaming at me for knocking a green bean off my plate at a dinner had crossed my mind leaving me stunned.

The night ended up being the nicest I'd had in the apartment since I moved in. The awkward tension between the two of us had diminished and I ignored my body's desire for him.

We ended the night with a movie and a smile, but the most challenging part was going back to my bed alone when I wanted to beg the man I shared the apartment with to join me.

CHAPTER TWELVE

CHANCE

Keeley and I had gone back to normal, sort of. Sex seemed off the table, which was devastating to my cock because he desperately wanted her. And no one else either, for that matter. Besides helping me study twice a week to make sure that I was staying on course, Keeley and I bickered like old roommates and even got back into the habit of binge-watching shows together.

I also thought her growing friendship with Darla was amusing and liked to remind her that I'm the reason that they met in the first place.

The downside of Keeley and I keeping our distance, besides not finding anyone worth fucking, was that my nightmares had returned with a vengeance. I hadn't had a good, solid sleep in weeks and I was starting to affect my work and how I played.

Turning to glance at my phone, the screen said it was only 2:15 in the morning and I had already been awake for an hour trying to make sense of the vision that continued to haunt me. The scene continued to play repeatedly, adding one minute detail every time. The only conclusion I could come up with was that it was a memory of some sort.

Closing my eyes, I tried to go back to sleep, but it eluded me. All I kept seeing was a little girl's face as she drove away.

Grabbing my phone, I used the search browser to determine why I kept having the same dream over and over again. I landed on a website that said the visions were suppressed memories and that I may have gone through some sort of trauma that blocked out that particular event. I wanted to believe that it was that simple because my entire childhood was one big traumatic event.

I tried to force the scene to play again for me, but nothing came. The memory only surfaced in the calmness of slumber.

Knowing that I was not going to be able to fall back to sleep, I swung my legs over the bed, dropping my head into my hands as my elbows rested on my knees. A stack of envelopes on the desk taunted me, laughing at my misfortune. I wanted to blame Keeley for my nightmares returning, but I was certain that the mail addressed to Elliott Winslow was the real reason.

Turning on the lamp on my bedside table, I stood and grabbed the cluster of envelopes. I already knew what most of them contained; I'd received a handful of these every year. I'd thought changing my address and name would make a difference, but it never did. She always knew how to find me; a maximum-security prison couldn't hold her back.

Opening the envelope at the bottom of the stack, I rolled my eyes at the first line: My dearest Elliott. The woman was a nut job if she thought that she could still have any claim over me.

My dearest Elliott,

I hope that this letter finds you well. I've started working with a special in-house therapist and she suggested that I needed to work through my regrets, the first being you. So, if it's okay with you, I'd like to continue writing you letters. I know that I don't deserve to have you read them, but maybe it would help me heal.

I wish that you would come to see me, Elliott. I miss you.

Love,

Mom

Balling up the letter in my fist, the crackle of the paper did nothing to diminish my anger. In rapid-fire succession, I tore through the other envelopes, each one my mother discussing her need to make amends so that she could lose her guilt. Each one she ended with her begging me to visit.

All of them were about her. She never considered how her actions had affected me or how I had to change everything about myself to disassociate from her actions. She had changed my life and she was hoping that I could just turn a blind eye and let her back in my life.

I'm not sure how long I sat in my room staring at the individual slips of paper with their jagged edges as they scattered across my bedroom floor, but the darkness of the night outside my apartment window gave way to the light of day.

The world did a great job of imitating my life. Clouds filled with rain hovered low, blocking most of the sunlight. The air was dull and lifeless outside. Dark and dead inside with the serrated edges of fury.

After collecting the pieces of my past in a plastic bag, I carried them to the kitchen to toss it in the trash. At the same time, Keeley bounced out of her room with a grin so wide it could outshine the sun.

"It's a great morning, isn't it?"

"Great, isn't quite the word that I would use. What has you in such a good mood?"

"I don't know. Life, maybe. Or the fact that I get to check a couple of other things off my list today."

"Really? What kind of things," I asked curiously. I made the two of us some scrambled eggs and bacon out of habit. I cracked a couple of eggs in a bowl and tossed in some crème fraîche.

"Well, I have an appointment for a tattoo and piercing this morning."

As I scrambled the eggs in the pan, she told me about the small heart tattoo she planned to get on her hip, but she clammed up when I asked about the piercing.

"What kind of piercing are you thinking of getting, Keeley?"

"I want something hidden, so. . .I don't know. . .I was thinking of piercing my clitoral hood or a nipple. Something only I would know was there."

Serving our breakfast, I carried the plates to the bar top counter and sat beside her. I couldn't help but notice that Keeley squirmed on her stool as I inched mine closer to hers.

Leaning toward her, I brushed my lips across the edge of her ear as I whispered. "Maybe rethink the piercing, little mouse. That pussy is mine and it's perfect the way it is."

Her cheeks turned that beautiful shade of pink that I grew so fond of.

She licked her lips. My eyes were drawn to the subtle movement. "What about the other option?"

"It would be hot as fuck for you to have your nipples pierced, but you'll have to go weeks without them being touched. And if I remember correctly, you enjoy having your nipples sucked."

She seemed to consider what I was saying based on the contemplative look she had in her eyes, or maybe she was considering a way to kill me. It was hard to say.

Keeley pushed the plate away with the breakfast I had made her and grabbed her purse that sat on the little table by the entry.

"Well, I don't think I need to worry about the consequence of either action, do you, Chance?"

The door slammed behind her, and I pushed aside my own breakfast, my hunger long forgotten. She was right. I had zero say in what she did with her body, and though I always enjoyed a few body modifications, her body was perfect the way that it was.

My phone rang and I grabbed it from my back pocket, ready to decline since I wasn't expecting a call, but the number flashing on the screen had me second-guessing.

"Hello?" I said in greeting.

"Can you meet me in ten minutes at the coffee shop on Main Street?"

"Sure."

The call ended as quickly as it had started and it left me reeling. Did someone find out about me? Was it the university? Tracy had assured me that nothing would be amiss, but there was always that fear that my past would destroy my future.

I dashed out of the apartment and got to the coffee shop in record time but then found myself pacing just outside the entrance. I still never felt like I deserved this chance at a new life. There was always the guilt that I'd found some sort of happiness while others didn't.

"Chance?" a heavy Bostonian accent called out and I turned to find my adoptive father, Adam's, old coworker. Link had been imperative about keeping in touch with Adam's cop buddies after his passing. Brent Daughtry had left the field but continued as a private investigator on contract.

"Brent," I said as he hugged me. He was a father-like figure in our lives and he stepped in when we had all lost that piece of our lives.

"I wish I saw you under better circumstances, but I have some. . .new information. Let's get something to drink and have a seat."

I followed him into the overly crowded coffee shop for a drizzly Saturday. Brent tried to make small talk in line, but I was too worried to do anything but grunt.

We found a small table in the corner and headed in that direction. Once we sat down, Brent plopped two manila folders onto the table, labeled C and K.

"I was going to ask if the information was about Keeley or me, but I think you just answered that question." Grabbing the folder on top of the pile labeled C, I began flipping through the pages. "Why do you have this information on me? Was someone asking about it?"

"No, this is the information Adam gave me and I've kept on hand. I thought that it was time that you had it. I'm sure it's not anything that you didn't already know, but there may be a few surprises."

Nodding, I reached for the other folder and began to open it before Brent's large hand landed on top, halting the motion.

"I want you to know that there is a lot of information here that is damaging and there will be severe ramifications if it falls into the wrong hands. There is also a good chance that your friend has no idea about any of this."

"By the way you're talking, I can already tell that she doesn't."

"Go over everything slowly and thoroughly, but don't do anything rash because that knowledge is going to destroy more than just one life."

"I'll make sure to read it carefully."

Standing, Brent placed his hand on my shoulder and squeezed gently. "Good luck, kid. And just remember that you have a big family that loves you."

He left without a backward glance and I remained sitting in the wobbly chair in the corner, watching people trickle in and out of the coffee shop but not actually seeing anyone. I had two folders in my hands that could change the course of everything. It was a power that no one deserved to have.

Contemplating whether to open them or not, I stood and turned to leave when I noticed Keeley bounce into the shop with Sarah trailing behind. Both women were laughing as they approached the counter. As if she could sense my presence Keeley turned and we made eye contact. She looked so carefree and innocent, and I was simply a smudge that dirtied her up. I don't know why I ever thought that she was plain and ordinary; she was anything but. Keeley was the bright light in my shadows and I wasn't sure that I could risk dimming that light.

With a smirk, I acknowledged her and then left the coffee shop, wishing I had brought an umbrella to combat the heavy rain that started to fall. Tucking the folders into my waistband, I ran back to the apartment, ignoring the sting of the rain as it fell against my arms. Thankfully the rain was warm, the remnants of a late-year hurricane from the south, and it didn't chill through my bones like a winter rain could. Though I would welcome the chill of the cold, it's the only time I felt anything.

A new envelope addressed to Elliott goaded me in the apartment as I passed it and went for the couch, placing both folders on the wooden coffee table.

My eyes darted between the C and K on the label, moving back and forth like a ping pong ball. The large C called to me, knowing that the past I longed to forget was just a few inches away. But instead of listening, I reached for the folder marked with a K. The moment my eyes scanned through the first page, I knew that I had made a mistake, but there was no chance of me turning away.

RENEE HARLESS

CHAPTER THIRTEEN

KEELEY

Sarah and I sat in the coffee shop sipping an iced chai tea latte. She had gone with me to get the small heart tattoo on my hip and surprisingly agreed with Chance about the piercing. It was the first time we had spent some time together, just the two of us since she screwed up the apartment renewal. Sometimes I liked to think that it worked out for the best, but there were other days when I couldn't figure out if the anger Chance ignited in me was worth it.

I listened to her discuss her and Archer's plans after her graduation next year, but I wasn't really hearing anything. Sure, I smiled and nodded at all of the appropriate times, but I wasn't very vested. Truthfully, I was jealous. I wanted the happiness that she and Archer shared. It seemed that particular outcome wasn't in the cards for me. My life was heading toward a bleakness of corporate monotony.

"Keeley?" Sarah said and I jumped in my chair as I was startled.

"Sorry."

"You weren't even listening to me," she said with a sad smile.

"I was lost in my own head. I didn't mean to zone out."

"What has you so distracted? Is Chance still giving you a hard time?"

I hadn't told her or Jolee about the few times Chance and I had fucked. They were dating his brothers, so I figured they wouldn't want to know. I also assumed that the girls would tell me that it was a bad idea. Chance had a reputation for a love 'em and leave 'em guy with a bad attitude. His reputation was precisely that, but there were moments where he gave me a glimpse of the Chance he kept locked away.

"No, not that. I'm just trying to figure out if I'll submit my form to graduate early or hold out. My dad is pushing me to take over this year."

"Why is he pressuring you so much?"

Shrugging my shoulders, I took a sip of my drink. I didn't have an answer, though I was a bit curious myself. His call last weekend had been completely focused on my classes and the credits I needed to graduate. He ignored my questions about the pressure and why I couldn't stay one more year. Mom hadn't even wanted to speak to me, which hurt the most. She'd only taken a call from me once since the semester started. Things weren't adding up.

"Wow, it's coming down," Sarah added as she twisted in her chair and looked out the window. The rain was falling in thick, heavy sheets making it nearly impossible to see across the street. I thought about Chance rushing back to whatever his destination had been in this mess and whispered a secret prayer that he got there safely.

"Archer is waiting for me outside. Do you want a ride?"

At first, I'd planned to turn her down, but it was quite a trek back to the apartment and I did not want to risk crossing the street in this mess. I took her up on the offer and we exited the shop, standing under the awning until Archer walked over with two umbrellas in hand.

The drive took twice as long because most people couldn't drive in this weather. I was thankful that I wasn't the one behind the wheel. I thanked them both for the ride as I slid out of the backseat, promising that we would get together before fall break.

Taking the stairs up to the apartment, I was always apprehensive. I never knew which Chance I was going to encounter. Luckily when I made my way inside, Chance was nowhere to be found. Grabbing a water bottle, I skipped to my room and started to tug off my shirt until my notebook caught my eye. With the warm rain outside, I knew that there was one more item I could check off my list today.

"Chance!" I shouted as I stood near his door. "I have one more item I can check off my list today. Did you want to come?"

I was expecting him to answer, but he startled me when the door to his room flung open. He wore a sour expression and I found myself taking a step back.

But instead of the vile words he tended to use when he was in one of his moods, he shook his head. "Maybe next time."

"Is everything okay?"

"Yeah. . .I just. . .coach is on my ass. That's all."

"I'm sorry. I'd offer to help, but we both know that would be a disaster. Anyway, I'll catch you later."

Wordlessly he shut his door, leaving me standing in the middle of the hall confused and out of sorts. I'd seen many sides of Chance, but a somber one was new and a bit alarming. As I made my way out of the complex, I continued to wonder what had caused him to look so downtrodden.

The rain continued to pour in heavy panes, but the warmth lingering in the air didn't dissipate. Taking a deep breath, I walked out into the shower, letting the rivulets of water wash over me. I continued to walk until I reached the large courtyard across from the apartment parking lot.

Tilting my head back, I stood with my arms out, soaked everything in, and cried. I cried for the life I was being forced to have. I cried for the little girl that never felt wanted or loved. And I cried for the love I felt for a man that could never return it. Because somewhere in the midst of the fighting and fucking, I fell for Chance. I saw a side of him he never exposed to anyone else. There was love in the meals he cooked for us, in the movies he let me choose, in the extra hot water he let me steal for a bath. It was all there, even if he didn't know it.

"Keeley?"

Spinning around, I turned to find Chance approaching, wet shaggy brown hair dripping water onto his face.

"What are you doing out here?" he asked once he got close. The corners of his mouth and eyes were pinched as if he were worried.

"Well, I wanted to dance in the rain. Figured this was the best opportunity I was going to get."

"How can you dance without music?"

Spinning like a ballerina, I yelled over the sound of the rain hitting the ground. "I don't need music."

Closing my eyes, I continued to spin and weave around, letting my body move to the beat that pulsed through my head until I felt a hand on my shoulder halting my dancing. Without missing a beat, Chance placed a wireless earbud in my ear and the sound of an operatic ballad pulsed through the speaker. I glanced up to find that he had one in the opposite ear.

Chance guided my arms around his neck while he placed his on my waist, then gently, we began to sway to the music. With the rain falling around us, I felt like I was in a glittered snow globe.

A crack of thunder sounded off in the distance, but neither of us made a move to pull apart. I tossed my head back and laughed, knowing that it was probably less unsafe to be out here in a pending thunderstorm than it was to fall in love with Chance.

I turned my head to face my dance partner and was surprised to find him smiling. It wasn't that cocky smile he gave women that had them falling at his feet. No, it was that secret smile that only I'd witnessed.

As I smiled back the song ended, but Chance continued to hold me close. One of his hands moved from my waist to cradle the side of my face. Instinctively my face tilted into his touch, yearning to feel his warmth.

"Keeley," he sighed as he leaned forward, then he captured my lips with his own. I welcomed his kiss with a stroke of my tongue against his lips, begging for entrance. Our tongues teased their own dance as he met my strokes.

God, I was addicted to him. I wanted to feel my body wrapped up in his like my own personal blanket. Chance made me feel safe and wanted. It was something I wanted to savor because I knew that it was all going to be taken away in a few short months. The memories would be all I had.

The moment was like something out of one of those romance movies I'd binge-watch with Sarah when we were feeling low. But it all shattered when my phone rang. I reached into my back pocket to silence the ringer with the hopes of going back to kissing Chance, but when I saw my mother's number on the screen, I knew better than to ignore it.

"Sorry," I mouthed to Chance, whose expression had morphed from sweet to callous. His lips were pointed downward in what looked like disappointment and he crossed his arms against his chest.

"Hey, Mom," I said, only to hear my father's angry voice on the other end snatch it from her. "Dad, what are you doing? Where is Mom?"

I tried to listen to what was happening on the other end of the phone, but the noises were too muted for me to make out their conversation. All I knew was that my mom had made the call without my father's permission, which was a big no in our house. My father controlled everything.

"Dad?" I tried again and he finally responded by telling me that he expected to see me at home next week for the break to discuss handing the business over. The call ended abruptly and I was left stunned while standing in the rain, glancing at my phone still in my hand.

"Keeley? What's going on?" Chance's hands framed my face to get my attention, but my mind was sifting through whatever had been taking place on the other side of the phone call. I'd never been worried for my mom's safety before, but that was before now. I'd never heard my father raise his voice at her in that way.

"Uh, that was my dad. Sort of."

"Sort of?"

"Yeah. I mean, my mom called but my dad freaked out because she didn't ask permission to use the phone. Then he said he would see me for fall break."

"I'm sorry, what? He restricts your mother's phone use? She's a grown woman. Who does that?"

"Someone that makes all the money and provides for us. Growing up, we all had to abide by his rules."

"And you want to return to that? Keeley, don't be stupid."

If he had slapped me, it would have hurt less than his words. Being called stupid was one of my triggers from childhood. I remembered being told over and over again that the only way I was going to amount to anything in life was to keep my grades high. My father didn't want anyone stupid associated with him.

I took a step back and then another until I ran at full sprint. I had no destination in mind, but I knew that Chance was following me without looking back. I could always feel when he was close.

The library came into view and I took the steps two at a time, slipping along the way but catching myself on the railing and propelling myself further.

"Keeley, stop!"

It was Saturday, but there were still students studying for their midterms in the library. The ones on the main level all turned their eyes to me as Chance continued to call my name.

"Geez, Keeley. Will you think this through really quick?" Chance said as he grabbed my arm and twisted me around to face him. "Your father is not who you think he is and you're making a very idiotic decision to work for him."

"Stop. He may not be the nicest man, but he's still my father. And forgive me if I am okay with the future he has planned out for me. That's more than I can say for you. You have no plan. You have no future, Chance."

"Jesus, Keeley. The man trades women and drugs. That's what your father does for a living."

"You're lying."

"Am I? Ask yourself why he's never told you what the business does? Why you've never seen any of his employees? Or why he keeps you and your mother under lock and key? Your father deals with the lowest of the low and you plan on blindly following in his footsteps. Except you're just a pawn in his elaborate game. Do you understand what I'm telling you, Keeley? Your father deserves to be in jail."

I couldn't listen any longer. I ripped my arm out of his hold and stomped away, ignoring the fact that one hundred or so people just heard the dirty laundry Chance just aired out without a second thought. None of what he said could be true. My father was a loving man that just wanted the best for my future.

He couldn't be what Chance accused of him.

The walk back to the apartment was a blur. I didn't even remember sliding my key into the lock or packing a bag. I had never been so angry or embarrassed, it was like my body was on fire and something kept feeding the flames. There was no escaping it.

There was something venomous slithering inside me and before I could take a second to question my actions, I left my room and headed down the hall. With a quick glance over my shoulder to verify that I was alone, I reached out and opened the door to Chance's room. Was it an invasion of his privacy? Yes. Did I care at that moment? Not in the least. The knob felt odd in my hand as if something possessed my body and actions.

Glancing up as I entered just incase Chance had rigged up some trap, I breathed a quick sigh of relief when nothing happened. I wasn't sure what I was looking for, but I needed something to get revenge for his words. I considered stealing one of his sweatshirts or taking all of his boxers, but then a manila envelope on his desk drew my eye. More specifically, it was the picture of me in a glossy 8x10 print that caught my attention.

Grabbing both folders, I made my way back to my bedroom and shoved them into my bag. I wasn't sure where I would go, but I knew that I couldn't stay with Sarah or Jolee. Luckily my friend Colleen had space on her couch until fall break began on Wednesday.

By the time I arrived at her apartment on the other side of campus, I was soaked to the bone, but I'd felt nothing. I was on the verge of a breakdown and Colleen was kind enough to make me a cup of hot chocolate while she listened to me vent about my problems. I tried not to be specific, but word about my father's rumored business deals had already circulated back to her. For the first time, I was the talk of the school and it was for all of the wrong reasons.

CHAPTER FOURTEEN

CHANCE

I'd screwed up royally when I aired out her dirty laundry to a massive group of people on campus. It was one of those moments where I'd lost myself in my need to protect her, and I honestly thought that was what I had been doing. But as I got back to the empty apartment an hour later to the knowledge that she was now the number one topic of the students, I realized my mistake.

My little mouse didn't want to be the center of attention and I just shined the spotlight on her. It was hard enough for her around campus because she lived with me. Girls gave her a hard time consistently. But this was an entirely different ballgame.

I grabbed my phone from my pocket the moment I entered the apartment, sighing when I noticed that the song we'd danced to was still playing on repeat. God, how did I fuck up such a beautiful moment with her? It was that damn phone call from her mother and Keeley's reaction to it. I had no idea what was said on the other end, but I could tell by her expression that it wasn't good. And when she mentioned still taking over her father's business, I exploded.

And I was filled with regret, but only for the way I ended up spilling the secret. She deserved to learn everything privately, not in the busy library. She deserved better from me.

My heart broke knowing what she was going through and then realization struck. My heart felt like it was crumbling because I pushed away the girl I had fallen in love with. And I was sure that there was no way to fix it.

Walking into her room with my phone in hand, I noticed that she had cleared out her dresser, the drawers pulled open and empty, but her bedding was still in place. At first, I thought maybe she just needed some time to think things over, but her desk was clear and she had taken that little bucket list notebook. I had grown so fond of it.

Because of my big mouth, I'd lost her before I'd even had her. And as much as I wanted to blame her father and his misgivings, I could only point the finger at myself.

Pressing Archer's number, I asked him if Sarah had been in touch with Keeley, which she declined. They'd both heard the rumor spiraling around campus and when I confirmed it, Sarah promised that she would track down her friend and talk to her.

Now, not only did I have to worry about my heart breaking, I had to worry that Keeley was safe.

I tossed my phone on my bed then stared out the window as the rain continued to fall. I wanted to drown in it, end this miserable existence that I had made up.

My thoughts drifted to the information I found in her folder. I hadn't even had a chance to skim through mine before I saw her spinning outside in the rain across from the complex. She had looked so happy and I was this cancer sent to annihilate it.

Knowing that I needed to give her the information Brent had found, I went to my desk to find the missing folders.

"Oh shit," I said to no one as I scrambled, turning my apartment upside down in search of the files.

She took them. Whether as an act of vengeance or to verify the information I had given her or simply out of curiosity, she had taken them.

God, I'd hoped that she wasn't reading them alone somewhere. I couldn't imagine the devastation she would feel at all of the information presented to her. Even as an outsider, I could barely process everything there.

I'd wished that Sarah would call back soon with Keeley's location so that I could help soothe her, but as the day turned into three, I knew any chance of things going back to normal was null and void.

That was until I grabbed the school paper in the cafeteria on the Tuesday before fall break and saw my name in bright, bold headlines.

CHANCE FINCHER IS ELLIOTT WINSLOW, CHILD METH CHEF

She'd done the unthinkable and exposed me to the world. The kids that read this paper were the same kids that had parents that were politicians, drug kings, and mafia legends. Hell, even princes and princesses of small countries attended Wellington and they now knew that I was the kid in one of the most heinous homicide, drug, and child endangerment stories to rock the country.

I skimmed through the article though I already knew what it would say. I knew about my past. About how my mother had taught me at the age of three how to cook down meth and package it in our small rundown house tucked away beside an apartment complex notorious for drug dealings. About how she had killed my father to pay a debt she owed. About how she abandoned me for weeks before the feds came to find me cooking the drugs she had ordered me to make. I was only allowed food when I met a certain quota. Elliott Winslow was the name I had left behind as I shuffled from foster home to foster home, running away from any hint of my past until Tracy had adopted me.

Everyone knew who the child meth chef was. There were even movies that depicted my story.

Somehow I had made it to the closest trashcan and got sick before anyone could begin asking questions. I wasn't sure how long I stood there heaving, but a soft hand on my shoulder offered the solace that I needed.

Tracy and Link stood on either side of me while Ford and Tyler positioned themselves as a shield while I composed myself as much as I could. Together, we walked out of the cafeteria and off campus as one unit.

The drive to Tracy's house had passed in a blur, and before I knew it, I was sitting in the same spot on the couch where Tracy and Adam asked if they could adopt me. It felt strange but full circle at the same time.

My family didn't bat an eye when I balled my fists up in my hair and screamed. They didn't look the other way when I asked why Keeley would do this to me. They didn't run off when I threatened them for just being there. They stayed because that was what family did.

I aired out my grievances. Spit spewing from my mouth as I described the last interaction with Keeley, my little mouse. She was so unassuming, but she needed retaliation. Only she didn't realize that damage she'd caused in her wrath.

Link stepped out of the room with his phone pressed against his ear, while Archer arrived a moment later with a girl that I didn't recognize trailing behind him, looking as though she wanted to be anywhere else.

I ignored them both as my phone rang and I recognized the number for my academic advisor. Tracy took the empty seat beside me and patted my knee, reassuring me that we would face this head-on.

"Hello? Yes, this is Chance Fincher." As my advisor began asking questions about the validity of the story posted, I said, "Yes, sir. It's true due to my involvement in my mother's trial.

"No, sir. My legal name was not changed until recently. The birth certificate and school transcripts were falsified to protect my identity per social services recommendation.

"Yes, sir, I understand. Thank you, sir."

A heavy sigh released as I ended the call, noticing the newcomer squirming in place but not making eye contact. I was put on probation while the school determined the ramifications for my falsified documents placed with my school application. I explained the conversation with the group and Tracy immediately went on defense.

"I will make sure you stay in school. None of this is your fault and it shouldn't be held against you. You were a child, for goodness' sake."

"I know, but falsifying legal documents is a crime, Mom."

Silence fell across the room for a minute, the grandfather clock chimed on the hour breaking through the tension.

Archer cleared his throat and introduced the newcomer. "This is Colleen. Keeley has been staying with her. She has something she wants to say." Her name was familiar.

I wasn't sure why the girl looked so nervous, but she seemed as sick as I had been earlier. Asking about Keeley's well-being was on the tip of my tongue before the girl blurted out that she had done it.

"Done what?" Link asked as he came back in the room with a satisfied look on his face. Or so I thought. Link was so stoic it was hard to determine how he was feeling based on his expression.

"I was the one that published the article. I run the paper and Keeley helps me with the advice boxes. When she came to stay with me, she went on and on about you ruining her life lying about her father's business. She said that she had found folders with information on both of you, and I took a selfish and opportunistic chance to sift through them.

"I thought I was protecting my friend. She's in love with you and you completely upended her world. So, I thought payback was fair play. I didn't think through my actions until the paper published this morning."

"Why would you do such a thing?" Tracy asked for me because my mouth had gone entirely dry.

"Notoriety? Revenge for a friend? Readership? I don't have an answer. I'm just a budding journalist that saw a chance to write a story. I'm only sorry that I didn't think of the consequences beforehand.

"I am truly sorry that this may have you expelled from school."

"It's not just that, dear, this article could put his life in danger. There are people out there that remember him and his mother. They still want retribution for various reasons."

There was a sense of victory as her face paled, but it only lasted a second. The damage had been done and I wasn't sure that there was ever any going back.

Could I create a new identity? Sure, but that would require me to leave my family behind and Tracy and my brothers were not something that I would budge on.

"I understand," I said, my voice hoarse from the earlier episodes.

"You do?" Colleen asked, her eyes widening twice their size in surprise.

"You made the choice because you thought you were helping a friend. Sometimes we don't think about how it affects the other party until hindsight hits."

She nodded, her blonde curls bouncing against her shoulders, giving her a youthful look, and I realized that she probably had never experienced something as extreme as Keeley and me.

"I really am sorry. I can't retract the story at this point, but I want to do whatever I can to help. I can even talk to the dean to make sure that you're not expelled. He owes me a favor."

Leaning forward, I rested my elbows on my knees and turned back to face Colleen. Tracy's gentle hand trailed up and down my back in support.

"You said that she loves me?"

"Yes. Keeley never said the words, but I could tell how devastated she was in the way that she spoke. She cried that entire first night and then decided to leave to stay with her parents. And I'm sure you know that she would never skip classes unless there were a good reason." Shamefully she looked down at the hardwood floors and scuffed the tip of her shoe against it. "I. . .uh. . .read the first couple pages of her file too, then I did some digging. I'm worried about her and what will happen while she's home. And for what it's worth, I would have done the same thing as you if I had learned what her father did."

From the corner of the living room, Link chimed in, saying that he had already alerted Brent to give the police department the go-ahead to infiltrate the Fox Trading company. We all turned our attention to the tall, long-haired man in the corner and watched as a devious smile grew on his face. He simply shrugged his shoulders.

"If you think I didn't already know about her situation, you'd be wrong. The minute Jolee and Sarah came into the picture, I pulled a file on her. And I'm glad that I did."

Tracy tsked at him as I turned back to Colleen.

"Thank you for coming here and confessing. I may need your help to settle things with Keeley."

"Absolutely, I'll do whatever I can to help."

Tracy made a full meal for everyone, not even allowing me in the kitchen. Colleen left shortly after I gave her the rundown of my plan while Jolee and Sarah arrived an hour later with sad, sympathetic smiles. Jolee even brought her dog, Balboa, a one-eyed mutt, to cuddle with me while we waited for the food to finish.

The sun was dropping below the horizon. I worried that neither Jolee nor Sarah had heard anything from Keeley except for a message that she was safe at home. They seemed to be just as worried as I was. I hated that I was stuck here while she was nine and a half hours away.

The girls cornered me in the living room after the late lunch and asked a hundred questions about me and Keeley and whatever our relationship was. I tried my best to make it sound better than it was, but really we were roommates that had grown into lovers that used arguing as our foreplay.

After the meal my brothers trickled out, leaving me with Ford, Jolee, and Tracy. We played with the dog for a short time until Ford sensed that I had something to tell him.

He looked at me expectantly and I caved once Balboa cuddled up against my leg. "I think you and Keeley may be related."

"What?" Jolee shouted, startling the puppy resting at my hip while Ford looked at me dumbfounded.

"In the paperwork Brent gave me, there was a birth certificate that listed R. Hastings as the father. No full first name, but I thought the coincidence was too strong to ignore it. Before I mentioned it to Keeley, I wanted to tell you first, though now I may never get that chance. Then I thought he may have told you already."

"Oh my gosh," Tracy and Jolee whispered in unison. Ford ran a hand down his face before tilting it toward the ceiling.

"Just talk to Brent to see if he can find out anything more, okay? I've rocked her world enough I don't want to give her information that may not be true."

Even though I wasn't sure she would believe me.

The couple gathered the dog that graciously licked my cheek before he was leashed up and walked out.

Tracy and I quickly worked on the dishes my brothers left in the sink. I was doing a shit job of drying, but my mother never said anything. She didn't even try to make small talk; Tracy just allowed me to process through everything.

"Can I stay here tonight?"

"Of course, Chance. You're always welcome here. I'll get you some clean sheets and a towel."

"Thanks, Mom."

"For what it's worth. I do think that you did the right thing in telling Keeley. Maybe not the way it happened, but it was better than you keeping the secret. Sometimes we're just not ready to hear the things we know may be true."

"I know that you're right. I just hate how it happened. She deserved better from me."

Tracy stared at me for a good while, her eyes assessing me in a way that only a parent can. I wished that she had been the only parent I'd ever had.

"Chance, do you ever wonder if there is a reason that you're drawn to Keeley? She's not your usual type, thankfully."

"I don't wonder, no. But I do feel like we are kindred spirits, like I know her from somewhere if that makes any sense."

"It does. I have something to show you."

Tracy guided me back to her office where she kept keepsakes from all of her kids' past lives.

"I realize that Brent gave you a copy of the file that Adam, my dearest husband, kept for you. Except it was missing a few things. Things that are going to make sense right now."

Tracy handed me a red folder and I laid it on the dark walnut desktop before flipping it over.

"There is a reason why you feel a connection with Keeley. You knew each other before coming to me.

"I'm sure the background of her story was in her file, but you were the one that alerted the police that she didn't know the woman that she was living with and had been wearing the same clothes for a week straight. Even amidst all the terrible things you were going through, you wanted to protect this little girl that needed help.

"This little girl had been your friend and you gifted her something that you found in your mother's belongings-," I quickly interrupted, glancing up from the file to look at Tracy as I said, "The necklace. She still wears it."

Reaching out, Tracy flipped the page and before my eyes was a photograph of a malnourished little boy and a dirty little girl, both with giant smiles that took up half of their faces. Despite their circumstances, they were both happy and carefree. And the piece of jewelry dangling around the girl's neck glistened in the sunlight.

Tracy's fingers ran across the picture before lifting the edge, folding the heavy cardstock, and facing me.

"Fate works in ways we'll never know or understand. It can devastate while it can exhilarate, but it has a plan. I don't know what that plan is, Chance, but it would be ungrateful to ignore that she was brought back into your life for a reason. With love, you can overcome anything and I've seen the change in you since this beautiful woman became your roommate."

"Do you think she'll forgive me?" I whispered as I tucked the red file under my arm.

"I think that she's more worried that you won't forgive her."

"Really?" I asked with hope filling my soul. That was all I had left to look forward to – hope for a better tomorrow.

"Why don't you ask her?" Tracy nodded toward the door where Keeley stood nervously, her hands twisting in circles around each other.

"Hi."

CHAPTER FIFTEEN

KEELEY

"Hi," I said with a nervous wave. I wasn't sure what kind of reception I was expecting, but Chance staring at me like he'd seen a ghost wasn't it. On the other hand, Tracy rushed forward and welcomed me with open arms. She was so warm and loving. Completely opposite of the two parents I'd had growing up.

"I'll leave you two to discuss things. I just want you both to remember that we are a product of our past, but it doesn't define who we are today. We get to make our decisions and no one else has a say."

Her words resonated with me after the long flight back from Vermont, where my parents purchased property on the Canadian border. If I thought Chance's words three days ago had thrown me for a whirl, that was nothing compared to the FBI breaking into their home and arresting both my father and mother on the spot just as I landed at the local airport.

The driver took me straight to the jail, where my parents were being booked and interrogated by a detective. The department didn't take any pity on me, but they did allow me to see my mother, who cried endlessly, repeating that she was sorry over and over again.

I still didn't understand until a man named Brent walked into the facility and asked for me. He quietly filled me in that he had been the investigator hired by Link, Chance's brother, and was the one that discovered what my father's business had truly been about.

I hadn't wanted to believe him, but he pulled out papers from his bag that showed copies of their financials and images of them completing the drug and shipping container exchanges. When I realized that those containers held people, I got sick in the room. I was pretty sure some of it landed on his nicely polished shoes.

Brent didn't take long to convince me to leave and travel back to Wellington. I did take a moment to look at my mother and tell her goodbye. She seemed remorseful that I was somehow wrapped up in all of this, but my father's sneer was the factor that blew it all up. He had hoped to escape all wrongdoing by passing it onto me. I was his scapegoat. My life meant nothing to him.

That was what Chance had been trying to explain, but I was too stubborn to listen.

I was ushered onto Brent's private plane just as Sarah emailed me a copy of the school's paper released that morning. The headline would have made me sick if I had anything left in my stomach. Colleen had betrayed me and now I knew Chance would never allow me to apologize.

"Keeley," he whispered with what looked like shock on his face after Tracy released me from her arms. Brent lingered in the hallway outside the door where the matriarch went to join him.

"Kelly is my name, actually. Or so Brent's paperwork tells me."

"You have to know I never meant for any of this to happen. I just wanted to protect you," Chance explained. His eyes met mine and we both silently pleaded for forgiveness.

"I'm sorry," we said simultaneously, both of us chuckling at the exchange.

"You don't have anything to apologize for, Keeley. Colleen came and confessed to writing the article in the school paper. She didn't realize the ramifications of her actions but promised to make things right."

"Make things right?" I asked, instantly regretting that I'd given Colleen the chance to learn anything about someone that they weren't willing to provide on their own.

"The dean has put me on probation for the time being until they can investigate more. The legal documents on my application were falsified to protect my identity."

A gasp escaped my lips as I threw my hands in front of my mouth. I'd never imagined the lengths someone would go through to protect themselves, but not it was something I was considering for myself.

"Chance, I'm so sorry."

"You don't have to be the one apologizing. That should be me. I should never have allowed my temper to react the way it did. Learning of your father's business should have been discussed behind closed doors."

"You're right. It was embarrassing to learn about the situation in front of other people, but I do understand that you were caught up in the moment."

Chance stepped away from the desk and walked toward me, where I hovered just inside the office. He gave the edge of the door a push, forcing it to shut, as he led me to a green chesterfield couch across from a dark walnut desk in the middle of the wood-paneled room. I would love to browse the bookshelves that lined the far wall during any other circumstances but now wasn't that time. Instead, I sat beside him, our knees brushing as we faced each other. In the three days, I'd almost forgotten about the electric current I felt across my body whenever our skin touched. It wasn't something I had been able to put into words when Colleen asked about my connection with Chance. It was just chemical.

"I want you to know that I didn't read the full file of the information Brent gave me. Just whatever had to do with your father."

"He was being arrested when I arrived." I went on to explain everything that happened at the airport and the jail, Chance flinching as I explained my father's harsh words toward me. "When I boarded Brent's plane, he gave me the second half of the file, which filled in all the missing pieces of my childhood. The things I never could remember."

Chance chose that moment to reach out and clasp my hands between his. It was just the strength that I needed at that moment to disclose everything that I was just beginning to understand.

"The flight was short, so Brent gave me some reading material. I was born Kelly Jean Vaughn to a Rose Vaughn and an R. Hastings. At least, that is what my birth certificate claimed.

"Just like you, my past was all over the news at some point. My mother sold me in a stroller to buy drugs, but they were undercover FBI agents.

"I was a preschooler at the time, and during the booking, one of the FBI agents took off with me before social services had arrived. She had been going through fertility treatment when her husband was killed in a drive-by shooting.

"From what I read, we moved across the country to a shady apartment complex where my caretaker got a job working at a laundromat being paid under the table. Somehow the local cops got alerted of our presence a couple of months later and they shipped me off to live with my aunt.

"I can't remember anytime before I came to live with my aunt and uncle. When I read Brent's file, it was like I was reading about someone else's life."

"What can I call you?" Chance asked, breaking me from the monotonous words that kept trickling through my vision. All those pieces of paper that Brent handed me were like dust in the wind.

"I don't understand," I whispered, looking down at my fingers twisting on top of my thighs. Chance reached over and settled my movements with his hand.

"Which name do you want me to call you, little mouse?"

I wasn't sure why, but the use of his nickname for me broke a dam I didn't know existed. My body crumbled forward as the turmoil of the last few days made itself known—arms wrapped around me as Chance shuffled me onto his lap, his body cradling mine in comfort.

"Shhh. . ." he murmured against my ear as he soothed me. Something about his deep voice and subtle rocking lulled me into a dreamless sleep once my tears had dried up.

Darkness bathed the room, and at first, I worried about where I was until I felt a strong arm tighten around me.

"Hey," Chance said against the back of my neck as he pressed his lips to the soft skin.

"Hey, where are we?" I knew this wasn't the apartment, but I couldn't remember much before I boarded Brent's plane to head back to Boston.

"We're at Tracy's in my old room."

"Oh. Are those your trophies?" I asked, taking in the space.

"They are. Most are from high school. A couple were from before I came to live here."

"Really?" I asked, settling against him and savoring the feel of his hands running through my hair as he leaned up on his elbow.

"Yeah. Some of my foster families kept them for me."

Turning in his arms, I adjusted my body to lay as close to him as possible. I wrapped an arm around his waist to keep him close. Tucking my head against his bare chest, I said, "I read the article. I had no idea you had gone through all of that, Chance. I'm so sorry that you were exposed that way. I didn't know what was in the folders when I grabbed them. I was just so angry and hurt at the time."

"Shhh. . ." he said, pressing his index finger against my mouth. "You don't need to apologize."

His question from earlier flirted with my memory and I smiled as I said, "Keeley. Call me Keeley, please."

"Okay, Keeley. When you're ready, I'm going to cook us some dinner and we're going to talk about a few things, okay?"

At my startled expression, Chance added, "Good things."

I watched as he strutted out of the room, those dimples above his ass hypnotizing me with each step until he was out of sight. Quickly I shuffled out of bed, thankful I was still fully dressed and made my way out of the room into the hallway. I realized that we were upstairs and followed my nose to the smell of freshly baked bread to find the kitchen.

Tracy was nowhere to be found, but I knew that she was the culprit for the baked goods.

"That didn't take you long," Chance chuckled as he wrapped his arms around me. None of this was the welcome I had expected. Truthfully I was still surprised that Tracy had allowed me into her house to begin with.

I had erupted a volcano of epic proportions, but she greeted me with a hug and a warm smile.

"I was hungry." Grabbing one of the rolls sitting on a baking dish, I hopped onto the counter, where Chance quickly pushed his body between my legs.

"I didn't read through all of your files. Just the first couple of pages related to your father. If there were anything you wanted to tell me about your past, I knew you'd tell me when you were ready.

"But Keeley, there is something that I need to discuss with you."

"What's that?"

"I want to tell you that. . .before I knew you. . .before my world was flipped upside down. . .I. . .ugh. . .Fuck, why is this so hard?" Turning his back toward me, Chance reached into an upper cabinet and grabbed a bottle of bourbon and a glass, pouring the caramel-colored liquid, then tossing it back like it was water.

"What's so hard, Chance?"

Spinning around with an angered expression, Chance shouted, "I fucking love you, okay? I love you."

"You love me?" I questioned, completely stunned by his outburst.

"That's what I said." Chance poured another shot and swallowed it just as quickly.

"Chance, I love you too."

With the glass hovering mid-air, he placed it gently on the table then set both hands on my cheeks.

"You love me? After everything?"

"I do," I reassured him as I leaned into him. "I realized that was why I was so upset about you telling me about my father's business. It had nothing to do with him but everything to do with you. I felt. . .betrayed."

"I don't know what to say other than I'm sorry. I never wanted anything like this to happen. I was just worried that your father was dealing with illegal outsourcing. I had no idea what he was working with."

"Chance?"

"Yeah?"

"Can you just kiss me now?"

"I can, but I have some other news that wasn't in the folders, Keeley."

Chance sunk his mouth against mine, savoring the kiss as if it were the last. Which only left me more worried than before.

"There are a few things about me that weren't in the folder, but it explains the connection that we have. Why there is this sense of familiarity."

For so long I had thought I was crazy, but Chance quickly put my mind at ease, knowing that he felt the connection too.

Chance explained that we were friends as kids, that part of my life that I couldn't remember. When I was taken, the apartment complex was next to where his mother sold her drugs.

He had been the one to call the cops on my kidnapper. He had been the one that protected me when the police arrived, sheltering me in the little cardboard clubhouse he kept in the woods behind the complex. He had been the one to steal the simple necklace from his mother's jewelry box and give it to me as a token of his friendship.

Even at a young age, I had known to treasure the small trinket, and now it meant even more.

Chance showed me the file Tracy had given him earlier and I couldn't dim the smile that bloomed on my face as I shuffled through the pictures of us as children.

Despite all of our past misgivings, fate gave us a second chance to make it right.

"What are we going to do, Chance?"

"Well, I say we get your things and head back to the apartment. I can't imagine my life without you, little mouse. Knowing you were such a big part of my past makes my future worth living."

"Chance," I murmured. "I'd relive it all if it guaranteed that we'd be together."

"Just no chasing me with bats." Chance chuckled against my mouth as he kissed me and I eagerly returned the favor.

"I make no promises."

RENEE HARLESS

EPILOGUE

CHANCE

"**T**hat's the last of it," I said as I carried the large cardboard box up the stairs.

Once news broke about my background and Keeley's, the school had waived the academic probation for the upcoming semester. Colleen, Brent, and Tracy had been critical in having us reinstated as students, but the dean had requested that the two of us complete our courses remotely.

Regardless of the school's change of heart, both Keeley and I decided to take the spring semester off. There were things that both of us needed to take care of and settle so that we could focus on school and ourselves. I continued to practice with the team since I had signed a guarantee that I would be returning and took the leave for personal reasons, but I couldn't play in any games.

"Thanks, babe. You can put it on the kitchen counter."

I kissed the top of Keeley's head as I passed. She was sitting with her legs crossed on the floor, sorting through some books she had taken out of storage.

We hadn't spoken much about her aunt and uncle's upcoming trial. They were being indicted on multiple charges, including homicide. We weren't sure of her aunt's full involvement, but from what we read, she had been critical in hiding evidence and the main person that pinpointed people of interest for trafficking. Keeley said that she wanted to leave that part of her life behind.

It still boiled my blood ever to think that man trapped Keeley. To think that she could have been sold off and sent away at any given point. And he had been using her all long. She was his means for escape.

During the initial investigation, millions in offshore accounts had been found along with properties worldwide where there was no extradition. The moment Keeley could graduate, he was taking off –

alone. He had no intention of taking his wife on the journey or protecting her.

But because Keeley's aunt had kept records on everything, they were going to spend a lifetime in jail.

She also created a trust for Keeley that included their estates in the US. It meant that Keeley wasn't going to have to worry about how she would pay for her tuition. The funds in the trust would stay there. Keeley wanted nothing to do with the dirty money, though she had appreciated the gesture. At least her aunt had wanted to make sure that she was cared for if ever the shit hit the fan. Keeley sold the properties, all three mega-mansions, and pocketed the funds.

That was enough for her and would allow her to follow her dreams of becoming a teacher.

The only unsolved piece of the puzzle was figuring out what had happened to her birth mother. Brent was on the case, but from what he had found so far, Senator Hastings had been instrumental in having her mother removed from the picture. Until we knew differently, we believed that he had hired someone to murder her. The man had a sordid background of his own that news reporters were just beginning to bring to light.

Senator Hastings had met his untimely death due to a heart attack the year before, just as Ford had learned that he had been his father. That left no concrete way to learn anything about Keeley's past.

I'd wondered if she was upset that there was no single person left from her family, but whenever I asked, she'd smile and say that she had her friends and me. That was all the family that she needed.

Except I knew what it was like to feel all alone, what it was like to feel like you had no one on which to rely. Keeley deserved more than what she had been given, she deserved the world, and I would do my damnedest to give it to her.

Even though my mother continued to reach out, I had zero desire to connect with her. I needed to move on and so did she. One night Keeley suggested that I write her one letter back, explaining how having her in my life was detrimental to my mental health.

We had Tracy read through it and I was surprised when she wrapped me in her arms after reading through the three-page letter where I gave my mother the current state of my life and let her know that I was happy and in love. That was all she needed to know and if my mother couldn't come to terms with how things worked out, then that was on her. My consciousness was clean.

"Do you want me to make some lunch?" I asked from the kitchen while peering through the open concept floor plan to watch Keeley immediately bounce up with a smile on her face. My girl was learning how to cook and loved the opportunity to try something new.

"Can I help?"

"How about you just sit your pretty ass right here and watch me?" I said as I lifted her onto the counter. This was my favorite place to have her. We'd only started moving our things into her new house down the street from Tracy's yesterday and I'd eaten her pussy and fucked her on the marble counters three times already.

She would always be my favorite meal.

With an adorable pout, she relented and watched me mix up a salad and then cook up some steak slices. Her feet swayed back and forth, her leg rubbing against my hip with each pass.

"You're playing with fire, little mouse," I told her as I turned off the burner on the oversized gas stove and moved to stand between her legs. Keeley's arms wrapped around my neck and I pressed my face against her exposed neck. The second her light perfume drifted across my nose, I immediately relaxed. The scent of Keeley was home to me.

Pressing my lips to the soft skin, I said, "Aren't you sore?"

"Yeah, but I don't care," she replied as she began gathering the material of my shirt and lifting it over my head. "I want you. Watching you be all domestic in the kitchen of our home does something to me."

I growl vibrated deep in my chest as my shirt fell to the floor. My hands slid around Keeley's legs to her ass and I gripped those round globes, lifting her. Keeley wrapped her legs around my waist as I carried her toward the stairs. The master bedroom was upstairs and there were a few new things that I wanted to try since we didn't have neighbors within listening distance.

My foot hit the first stair just as the front door flung open.

"Hey, we brought beer," the familiar voice called out and I rolled my eyes knowing that our quiet time together was about to be ruined.

Ford stepped through the front door with Jolee and my brothers trailing behind him when I placed Keeley down on the second step.

She mouthed, "Sorry," before sliding her hand over my erection then moving to greet the crowd standing in our foyer. The little mouse had turned into a minx. I was left standing there with my back to everyone while I named off random baseball players in my head to get my cock to stop standing at attention.

Finally, when I could walk without everyone noticing what Keeley and I had been up to, I walked through the living room back to the kitchen, where everyone was congregating. And where Ford was eating my salad.

He and Keeley were still coming to terms with the fact that they were half-siblings. Ford kept his distance, as he did with everyone, but I could see the longing in Keeley's eyes. He was her blood and she wanted a relationship with him. I tried to explain that he would need time, but the hurt still remained.

Sidling up beside her, I wrapped my arm around her waist and pulled her close. Without missing a beat, she speared her fork in the salad and held it up for me to taste. We continued to share the meal until her plate was empty and she set it back on the counter.

"Thanks, little mouse," I added as I pressed my lips to her shoulder.

The group stayed for a few hours helping to unpack boxes. Keeley and I fed them with homemade pizza and the beer Ford brought as we graciously thanked them. Then we were finally alone in the house that Keeley desperately wanted to make a home. A place she wanted to make new family memories.

For me, it didn't matter where we were living, as long as I had her to come back to. She made all the bad worth it because I got to have her in the end.

We had pasts that we wanted to forget, but they were what shaped us and made Keeley and me appreciate each day that we had together.

Laying in the massive California King bed that we purchased together, I wrapped my body around Keeley's. We were both spent after christening every room in the house, but we saved the bedroom for last. This lovemaking wasn't fast or hurried. We spent our time slowly exploring every inch of each other.

My fingers toyed at the necklace she wore, the delicate charm resting on her pale skin. The two hearts of our past were the hearts that brought us together.

"Do you ever think of what may have happened if Link hadn't found me hiding in the library?"

"I'd probably be a lonely bachelor living up the playboy lifestyle."

Keeley turned around with a frown on her face, noticing the smile I was wearing. She smacked my chest, then pressed her lips against the same spot.

"I'd be miserable. I was miserable until you were forced into my life."

"I feel like we probably owe Link a thank you."

"Naw, we would have found our way back to each other. The lies of our past weren't going to keep Fate from stepping in."

"Do you really believe that?" she whispered.

"After everything that happened, I absolutely know that we were meant to be together. Someway or somehow, our lives would have collided," I said as I twisted Keeley in my arms so that she laid on her back. I settled between her bent legs.

"I love you, Chance."

"And I love you, Keeley. Even though everything happened so fast, you've been part of my life for years. We are exactly where we're meant to be."

I watched her fall asleep against me with a small smile on her lips. I never worried about my nightmares any longer. After reading through all of the information Brent had compiled, I'd realized that they were memories bursting through. Though sad and shocking, they were a part of our history. We'd hope one day they would no longer make themselves known. But with Keeley in my arms, they happened less and less.

Brushing her hair to the side, I pressed a kiss to her cheek before settling my body behind hers, wrapping my arm around her waist.

Whispering into the darkness of the room, I told her, "You're going to be mine forever, little mouse."

STAY IN TOUCH

Newsletter: http://bit.ly/2WokAjS

Author Page: www.facebook.com/authorreneeharless

Reader Group: http://bit.ly/31AGa3B

Instagram: www.instagram.com/renee_harless

Bookbub: www.bookbub.com/authors/renee-harless

Goodreads: http://bit.ly/2TDagOn

Amazon: http://bit.ly/2WsHhPq

Website: www.reneeharless.com

ACKNOWLEDGEMENTS

Thank you to all of the readers and bloggers that shared their excitement for this book and series. I hope that Chance and Keeley gave you the love story that you were hoping for.

Patricia thank you so much for the late nights and long days. Without you this book wouldn't have been possible.

To my family, your support has meant more than you'll ever know. Writing while renovating and having a new baby was definitely not something that I expected, but seeing your beautiful faces every day made it all worth it. I love you all so much, every day.

ABOUT THE AUTHOR

Renee Harless is a romance writer with an affinity for wine and a passion for telling a good story.

Renee Harless, her husband, and children live in Blue Ridge Mountains of Virginia. She studied Communication, specifically Public Relations, at Radford University.

Growing up, Renee always found a way to pursue her creativity. It began by watching endless runs of White Christmas- yes even in the summer – and learning every word and dance from the movie. She could still sing "Sister Sister" if requested. In high school, she joined the show choir and a community theatre group, The Troubadours. After marrying the man of her dreams and moving from her hometown she sought out a different artistic outlet – writing.

To say that Renee is a romance addict would be an understatement. When she isn't chasing her kids around the house, working her day job, or writing, she jumps head first into a romance novel.

RENEE HARLESS